KAREN WALLACE

Raspberries
on the
Yangtze

Delacorte Press

Published by
Delacorte Press
an imprint of
Random House Children's Books
a division of Random House, Inc.
1540 Broadway
New York, New York 10036

Visit us on the Web! www.randomhouse.com/teens
Educators and librarians, for a variety of teaching tools, visit us at
www.randomhouse.com/teachers

Cataloging-in-Publication Data is available from the Library of Congress.
ISBN: 0-385-72963-4 (trade)
      0-385-90050-3 (lib. bdg.)

Manufactured in the United States of America

June 2002

10 9 8 7 6 5 4 3 2 1

BVG

To David, with love

One

It all began the day my brother and I decided to poison our mother.

It was a warm sunny summer morning. We got up early and ate Rice Krispies for breakfast. We went back upstairs, pulled our curtains and did a sloppy job making our beds.

But maybe I should introduce myself first. My name is Nancy. My brother is called Andrew. We don't look anything like each other. He's got dark hair and a long face. His greeny-brown eyes have a wary look to them. Not that Andrew gets into trouble much. Quite the opposite. The reason he's wary is he's always on the lookout for trouble so he can avoid it.

I don't look wary. My mother says I should try it sometime. Maybe she's right. I always seem to be in some sort of trouble. Not big tornado trouble, you understand. Just a few whirly gusts that always knock something over. And somehow it's always my fault.

That's another difference between Andrew and me. Things are never his fault.

Anyway, unlike my brother, I've got blond curly hair and blue eyes and my face is round and freckled.

In fact if you didn't know Andrew was my brother, you would never guess it. The only thing the same about us is that we're both tall. And we spend most of our time outside.

That's because of the woods and the river. You see, we live in the country in Canada. Actually we live in an old log cabin. You can tell it's an old log cabin because the logs are wide, not narrow, and they have squared-off ends that dovetail into each other. The space between the logs is filled with crumbling white mortar. When we first bought the cabin, it had two sticking-out bedroom windows with a red front door in the middle. It looked like it had a face that was smiling at me.

Anyway, then my mum and dad built a bit on the end to fit us all in so I guess you would call the cabin a wooden house now.

We live quite near a busy highway, but you'd never know that once you turn down our little gravel road. The house sits on its own at the end. There are pine trees in front of it. But behind it where the land slopes away there are maple and birch trees mixed in with the evergreens. There is a small lawn and there are flowerbeds around the house. In the summer Mum plants out red and pink geraniums, black-eyed daisies and blue and white forget-me-nots. A yellow rose is supposed to grow up one side of the house but something keeps eating it so it doesn't flower much.

Anyway, that morning my brother Andrew and I planned a trip down to the Gatineau River. The Gatineau is almost half a mile wide where we live. Each year, when the ice finally melts, it is a highway for thousands of logs floating downriver from the logging camps in the forests up north to the paper pulp mills further downstream towards Ottawa.

The part of the river we thought of as our own was a small backwater separated from the big river by a spit of land. Here there was no current and the water was only a few hundred feet across.

Every year a few logs always found their way around the spit of land and floated into our backwater.

Eventually, after a lot of hard looking, tough decisions were made and we chose two of them for the summer.

So that morning, Andrew and I were going to check on our logs.

Finding the right log is an important job. You start looking in May after the ice has melted and the log rafts start moving downriver. When you finally find the right one, you pull it up the stony, muddy bank as high as you can.

This year, after careful searching, I had found my best log ever. It was smooth, so you could ride it without the insides of your legs going all red, and not too long, so that it was easy to turn when you were paddling it. About a third of the way down there was a branch stub. It was a good shape. It could be a joystick. It could be the hilt of a sword. It could be the pommel of a saddle. It could be anything. It was the perfect log.

Andrew wasn't so fussy about his log. A log was a log, as far as he was concerned. But even so he had taken his time looking and finally found one that suited him. Whether he *liked* his in the same way that I liked mine, I don't know. The chances were with Andrew, he wouldn't admit to it even if he did. *Liking* your log would be sissy girl's stuff.

I thought of my brother as a deep thinker. I suppose this was because he always beat me at cards.

In the end, though, I think it would be truer to say that Andrew only pretended to be a deep thinker. He was really a dreamer. In his world, dreams and real things were barely connected to each other.

My dreams were part of my world. If I put on a pair of ballet shoes, I dreamed I was a ballerina. If I was trying to hatch out a bird's egg on top of my bedroom lamp, that bird was already my constant chattering companion.

At any rate, that morning as we slipped out of the back door my mother was cleaning and the vacuum cleaner sounded like a monster hornet on the rampage. It's funny how a machine can take on the mood of the person operating it. I mean, the vacuum cleaner could have sounded like a drowsy bumblebee on a summer's day. But it didn't. My mother was steering that vacuum cleaner like a rider from the gates of hell. I saw smoke pouring from her ears, her eyes burning with an unnatural green light.

"Did you tidy up your room?" muttered Andrew.

In my mind's eye I saw my bedclothes, half on, half off the bed. I saw my dolls' house open. Tiny dolls lay on the floor beside tables and chairs and waiting cars. There were also bits of material everywhere. I liked sewing and made little pictures out of fabric. And I had been cutting out the pieces for a birthday present for my grandmother.

The vacuum cleaner's roar got angrier. I could tell my mother was heading into my room.

"Come on," I said. "Before it's too late."

We followed a path behind the house down to a small rough meadow. It was always bright in the meadow because there were hardly any trees to block out the light. The grass was soft and thick and speckled with dandelions and yellow daisies. This was where we had our swings. We hurried on through a clump of birch trees, down towards the lower road where one of our neighbors lived.

Mr. Chevrolet was sitting outside. His house was also made of wood, but with overlapping planks, not logs. A bleached wooden verandah was fixed to three sides of the house which was built on the side of a valley.

Mr. Chevrolet was rocking gently on his battered pine rocking chair. He had a cigarette in one hand and a bunch of newspapers in the other. Mr. Chevrolet smoked Balkan Sobranies. Balkan Sobranies are Turkish cigarettes. They come in different colors in a cream and black box and lie in rows like exotic candy sticks on a bed of gold paper. Each day he smoked a different color. Today was Tuesday so I knew Mr. Chevrolet's cigarette would be one of the green ones with the gold band around the filter.

Mr. Chevrolet was Polish. We called him Mr. Chevrolet because we couldn't pronounce his last name so we decided to call him after the car he drove which was a Chevrolet. Besides, it sounded a bit like his real name. Mr. Chevrolet had laughed and declared that this was a fine solution to the problem and after a while we forgot his real name anyway. Mr. Chevrolet was like that. He liked to keep things simple.

I'm not sure what he did for a living. I think he

wrote books. I know he got parcels of books from all over the world. And he always steamed off the foreign stamps and kept them for us.

When he wasn't writing books, he fiddled with motorboat engines. Often it was the same engine. He spent hours coiling up springs and fitting them in place. And he never got angry when they jumped out and unwound around his feet, which they always did.

Mr. Chevrolet wasn't tall and skinny like my father. He was quite short and even a little bit pudgy. He had a smooth face with lots of white wavy hair. More than anything else he looked like everybody's idea of a perfect uncle. A perfect uncle who made homemade lemonade. There was always some in the kitchen and in the summer he would fill up plastic glasses if we looked thirsty when we were passing by.

We waved.

Mr. Chevrolet waved back and returned to his newspaper.

It was not going to be a lemonade day.

We followed the path down another steep hill and came out into the sun again. Railway tracks were in front of us. The line went from Ottawa up north to places we had never heard of. Only freight trains used it, and not many of them either. But even so, my mother had instilled in us a fear of being hit by a train. We had a drill we always followed. If we heard a train coming, we all stood on the same side of the tracks and waited as the huge iron monster clattered by. Both Andrew and I had tingling fantasies of jumping clear with seconds to spare, but there were so few trains we had pretty much given up on them.

We stopped and breathed in the hot sharp smell of creosote from the railway sleepers. Then as usual I walked balancing on one track and imagined it was a tightrope and I was an acrobat. Andrew strode down the middle, kicking up the white chippings between the sleepers.

Sometimes you saw striped green and yellow garter snakes sleeping between the tracks. One of our neighbors said she saw a wolf down here once. She got really near because at first she thought it was a big hairy gray dog. My mother said the wolf must have had rabies.

We were taught to be as frightened of friendly wild animals as we were of walking on slushy river ice in spring. So the story of the big hairy dog on the railway track was always a spine-chiller.

But today there were no wolves and no garter snakes. Andrew and I crossed the tracks and followed the narrow path that snaked through a wood of weedy maple trees down to the river.

I should say right now that we didn't start off with the intention of poisoning our mother.

It happened as we were lying on our stomachs at the end of the wooden jetty, staring into the murky water of the Gatineau River.

Two

I haven't mentioned this yet, but that morning Andrew and I had a lot on our minds.

Only two days before, Andrew had suffered a terrible humiliation.

It was in the morning and we were already late for the school bus. Just as we were leaving the house, it began to rain—heavy rain, that came out of nowhere and turned our narrow gravel road into a sticky white mess in five minutes.

"Boots on!" my mother ordered as we were halfway out the door. Her voice was muffled. We turned. All we could see was her backside poking out of the cupboard under the stairs. Then rubber boots began flying out at us.

I pulled mine on. I rather liked mine. They were red.

Andrew picked up his, sniffed them and pulled a face.

"Mum! I can't wear *these*!"

"Hurry up or you'll miss the bus," replied the backside.

"M-u-m!"

"Put-on-your-boots!" A low growl like a leopard. Or a rumble like a volcano. One of those volcanoes that are about to go all orange and hot.

"But M-u-m!"

Everything went hot and orange.

Our mother stood up to her full six feet. She had a square jaw and piercing eyes. Her dark brown hair was pulled back from her face in a loose ponytail. In another life, she might have led her Scottish clan into battle.

"A-N-D-R-E-W! PUT-ON-YOUR-BOOTS!"

"Bogey's pissed in them again!" wailed Andrew, holding up his boots by way of evidence. "They stink! I *hate* that cat!"

We had seven dogs and three cats. Bogey was a huge gray neutered tomcat. Bogey was mean and had it in for anybody and everybody. Most of the time he sat on the arm of a chair and waited with his eyes half closed until you passed near him. Then his great furry paw would shoot out like a snake and he'd clip you on the backside with his claws.

He also pissed in Andrew's boots. It was as if he had chosen them specially. Or put it this way, he didn't piss in anyone else's.

"Put them on *anyway*," ordered my mother. "You'll miss the bus!"

So he did and we trudged up the white gravel road

that led to the highway. Or rather I trudged, Andrew sort of squelched. I ignored the whiff of cat pee that swirled around his knees. It seemed the kindest thing to do.

The bus stop was on the other side of the highway. Four other kids used the same stop but none of them were there yet. Sandra and Tracy Wilkins lived on the same side as the stop. I could see their tidy white-shuttered house above me. Tracy didn't come on the bus with us anymore. She left school last summer and went to college in Ottawa which was about an hour away.

Amy and Clare Linklater were the other two kids. They were my favorites and they lived in a gray peeling house on our side of the highway.

Just as Andrew and I crossed the highway, they appeared out of the woods. Amy and Clare were allowed to wear what they liked to school. Amy wore a skirt on top of her dress and looked liked a gypsy girl. Clare wore a shirt and pants but she had cut off the ends of the arms and legs in ragged zigzags with a pair of rusty pinking shears.

We all said hi, but nothing more; after all, we saw each other every day. And even though we were good friends, our real friendship happened in the woods in the summer and had nothing to do with school and the trip in on the school bus. Especially as far as Andrew was concerned. He didn't want *anyone* to think he was a sissy just because he hung around with a whole lot of girls.

At this moment, Sandra and Tracy Wilkins trotted towards us. I guess maybe Tracy had a day off from college and was walking down with Sandra for something to do. I hadn't seen Tracy Wilkins for a while. She was small and slim with sharp features. She had become a dark-haired version of her mother. Her sister Sandra was pudgy and fair. For some reason Sandra was wearing the same clothes as Tracy— tight tartan pedal pushers. Pedal pushers didn't suit Sandra. Especially tartan ones. She looked like a pig that has sat on a waffle iron. Tracy, on the other hand, looked like something straight out of the young debutante section of a mail order clothes catalog.

As usual both of them wore dazzlingly white frilly blouses. Mrs. Wilkins's white things were always ten times whiter than anyone else's. Sandra had the whitest socks, the whitest petticoats and the whitest handkerchiefs. Since most mothers I knew couldn't wash things this white I was sure Mrs. Wilkins's *cleanness* had something to do with her working with the church all the time and believing in God so much. Put it this way, no other mothers took church as seriously as she did and the rest of us wore stripey socks and colored petticoats and didn't use handkerchiefs.

Once I was dragged along to a church barbecue run by Mrs. Wilkins. And before we could roast our marshmallows on the fire we all had to listen to her little talk. As far as Mrs. Wilkins was concerned, sins were dirty like the stubborn stains in detergent ads. They should be scrubbed away so no one could see them.

My mother once told me Mrs. Wilkins even wiped supermarket cans with disinfectant before she put them away on her shelves.

A little way from us, Tracy stopped and pushed Sandra forwards. "Bye, kid," she said with a foxy flip of her hair.

She was far too grown up to say hi to any of us.

"But you promised you'd wait with me," wailed Sandra. She sniffed and wiped her nose on her brilliant white sleeve.

"I don't keep promises to brats," replied Tracy in a snooty voice.

"But you promised *Mum*," wailed Sandra. "I'm *telling*."

The next minute Tracy twisted a handful of Sandra's wrist. "You keep your big mouth shut, you little creep," she muttered. Then she wiggled up the highway as if she was wearing high-heeled shoes instead of trainers.

Sandra shuffled towards us, sniffing. No one said anything. We had seen it all before.

At that moment the yellow school bus stopped with a squeal of brakes and a stink of old engine. We lined up to get in.

Andrew had been standing on his own, shifting from foot to foot and looking more and more miserable. Now he shuffled into line behind Sandra.

"Ugh!" said Sandra, sniffing and wrinkling her pug nose. "What's that *smell?*"

A few weeks back our School Principal, Mrs. Trimble, had introduced a new rule on all the school buses. Everyone had to mind their manners and be polite to each other. There would be no more shouting. There would be no more whacking heads with metal lunch boxes. Jimmy, a playground bully and the sort of kid who pulled legs off spiders and did worse things to frogs, had been put in charge on our bus. Mrs. Trimble had chosen wisely. Jimmy was just right for his job.

We started to climb up the steps on to the bus. Clare first, then Sandra, followed by Andrew, whose usual strategy for the Third World War ride to school was to hunch in the corner of his seat, speak to no one and stare out the window all the way.

At that moment, Sandra stopped to hitch the strap of her school bag over her shoulder.

It must have been the cat piss getting to him. Andrew broke the habit of a lifetime.

"Move along, slob," he muttered, with all the menace he could drag up.

That did it. Jimmy sprang into action with the glee of a mink surprising a rabbit. He pulled out his black book and carved a name inside it.

Andrew's doom was sealed.

During milk break, he was dragged up in front of Mrs. Trimble. His gold star for good behavior was unpeeled from his report card, crushed and thrown away.

It was, as I said, a terrible humiliation.

It was also, as our mother had pointed out all too clearly, the only gold star that Andrew was likely to get since lessons were definitely part of real life and as I said, with Andrew dreams came first.

Which was the reason Andrew was feeling wounded, hard done by and misunderstood as he lay on the jetty and stared into the murky water of the Gatineau River.

My own situation was completely different. I was confused, and it was all to do with cupboards.

I had recently developed a thriving business selling

the facts of life for fifteen cents to anyone who I thought should know them by now. It amazed me that mothers did not come clean to their daughters about these facts. I mean, what were they trying to hide? Everyone should know these things. They might be a bit weird, but so what? Once you got them in the right order, that was it.

Unfortunately, Sandra Wilkins's mother did not agree. As far as she was concerned, the facts of life were more stubborn stains. They did not belong in her house. Last night, she had called my mother demanding that I be gagged and Sandra's fifteen cents be returned forthwith. I knew this because I'd been hiding in my usual place at the top of the stairs just round the corner and had overheard the whole thing.

It wasn't the money that worried me. I had a growing list of customers as word spread of my knowledge and willingness to share it.

What worried me, as I too stared into the murky brown waters, was my mother's voice on the telephone.

"Cupboards?" she was saying. "I don't understand."

Well, I understood all right.

Sexual intercourse—the act of penetration of the female's body by the male organ—takes place in cupboards. That's why all bedrooms have them. That's what cupboards are there for.

Everyone knows that.

My mother's ignorant laughter rang in my ears.

Now I was beginning to worry whether even my own *mother* had her facts right. After all, it wasn't her who told me the bit about cupboards, I'd had to work that out for myself. It went like this. I knew you had to have a bedroom. But you couldn't do these weird things on *beds*—somebody might see you. So there's only one solution. And that's to jump into the cupboard. No one would see you in there. So really if there wasn't a cupboard near, nothing could happen in the first place.

So why hadn't my mother told me this? Perhaps there were other things she had left out, too?

On purpose to wreck my business.

"Jesus Christ!" shouted Andrew, who had taken to practicing swearing when we were on our own. "Look at that!"

He pointed down through the murky water.

I hung my head over the edge of the jetty and peered.

"Where? What is it?"

"There!" cried Andrew. "Jesus Christ! It's huge!" He pointed again.

And this time I saw it. It was a fish, lying lazily on the stony bottom. You could just make out its pale, wavering body in the dirty water.

"Let's catch it!" I whispered. We had never caught a fish before. In fact I had never seen one so close.

"Don't be stupid!" replied Andrew. "You can't catch it."

"Why not?"

"It's dead, stupid," said Andrew. "That's why it's not moving."

"How come it's not floating?"

Andrew rolled his eyes. "How should I know? Maybe it died, floated and sank again."

"Oh." I paused. "How are we going to get it, then?" For there was never any question of leaving it there.

Andrew looked thoughtfully at the pale wobbling shape as if he was testing various strategies. "I know," he said at last. "I'll hold on to your foot. You slide into the water and when you wiggle your foot, I'll pull you up."

That was usually the way round. I did the dirty sticky bits. Andrew did the masterminding. Like I said, he could always beat me at cards. Anyway, I don't mind dirty sticky things. And I was only wearing a pair of old shorts and a T-shirt.

I pulled off my trainers and lowered myself into the water. The fish was slippery and not easy to get hold of. In the end, I needed two hands. Finally, I got a grip on it and yanked my foot.

Andrew pulled me up and a moment later a big trout with a gash on the side of its head flopped onto the wooden deck.

We stared at our fish. Neither of us had ever seen one close up before. It had a dark green back with light green swirls. Tiny red and white blotches ran along its belly.

I stuck my finger inside its pulled-down mouth. Its teeth felt like a doll's saw blade.

Excitement fizzed in the air between us. We both knew this was the Adventure of the Fish Day. Something special had to be done about it.

Andrew bit his lip thoughtfully.

"It doesn't *look* dead," he muttered. "I mean it's not *rotten* or anything."

"It looks just like we caught it," I said slowly.

"Apart from the gash on its head," said Andrew.

As we walked back home, we decided on our story.

Andrew had found a piece of string. I happened to have a safety pin. We had baited the safety pin with a worm. We had caught a trout against all odds.

It was the most amazing thing that had ever happened to us.

And there was only one person who could be presented with such a trophy.

Our mother.

"Do you think it'll poison her?" said Andrew as we crossed the railway tracks.

I looked down at the cloudy golden eye of the dead fish in my T-shirt and shrugged.

Three

We strolled up to the swings in the meadow. Then we started to run.

"Mum! Mum!" I yelled as we crashed through the back door and into the kitchen. "We caught a fish! We caught a fish!"

"Good heavens!" cried my mother, not looking up. She was standing at the counter, bent over a lemon meringue pie. Her hair was wound into a roll at the back of her head. A few strands had escaped and hung down either side of her face. "Just a minute."

We watched the practiced flicks of her broad flat knife as she spread the sticky meringue in waves and swirls over the top of the pie. She always finished with a thick white curl in the middle. "How on earth did you manage that?" She tossed the knife into the sink.

"I had a piece of string and Nancy had a safety pin," explained Andrew, breathlessly.

He held out the fish.

I grabbed the *Joy of Cooking* from the shelf.

"You have to eat it now," I insisted. "It's fresh!" I

flipped the pages of the cookbook until I found the one I was looking for. "You have to roll it in flour first, then you have to fry it in a frying pan."

"We'll never catch one again," said Andrew, who was good at seeing things in their own place in time. "This will *never* happen again."

My mother laughed. "I've never heard of anyone catching a trout in that inlet," she replied. "Extraordinary. Here, give me the cookbook."

She looked again at the trout that gleamed on the counter. Some of its scales had already come off and stuck to the pinky brown marbled counter top. "What happened to its head?" She bent down and took the frying pan from its shelf under the sink.

"It wriggled so much Andrew had to hit it with a stone," I said.

"I found a special stone to do it with," added Andrew proudly.

"Extraordinary!" repeated my mother. Her face was flushed and she moved quickly around the kitchen. She was getting caught up in our excitement. She grabbed a bag of flour from the shelf and sprinkled some onto a plate.

"Get me an egg."

"Quick, Nancy!" cried Andrew. "Get Mum an egg!"

I whooped with delight as I rooted in the fridge. Nothing this exciting had happened for a long time.

"Wait till I tell Amy and Clare," I shouted. "They'll never believe it!" Because I really *was* beginning to believe it. We really *had* caught the fish with a piece of string and a safety pin.

I hopped from foot to foot.

Andrew stood with a wide grin on his face, basking in glory. He believed in our story, too. He was a real fisherman. It was *extraordinary*.

Meanwhile, my mother beat the egg with a fork and rolled the fish in it. Then she turned it in the flour.

We watched in silence as she lifted the limp floury body and dropped it in the frying pan.

We watched the fat fizzle and the fish skin puff up and go brown. We saw the tail curl and the body twist in the pan.

The kitchen filled with the smell of frying fish and something else we didn't recognize.

I looked at Andrew.

Andrew looked at me.

So much for the string and the safety pin. The truth filled the kitchen like the strange smell out of the frying pan. We had found a dead fish. It probably was rotten and now we were feeding it to our mother.

"Do you think she'll get sick?" I whispered. The word *gangrene* echoed round my mind, like a howl in a dungeon.

"I don't know," muttered Andrew.

My mother looked up. She must have thought we were disappointed.

"Maybe we should have gutted it," she said, sniffing guiltily.

The next minute she slipped the trout onto a plate and cut a small piece out of it.

Andrew and I watched with a mixture of horror and excitement as she raised the fork to her mouth.

What should we do? If she ate it, she'd get sick. She might even die.

If we told her the truth, everything would be ruined.

My mother opened her mouth.

Then she closed it and wrinkled her nose. "That's funny," she said. "It smells sweet. Trout shouldn't smell sweet."

Andrew and I looked at each other again.

"Oh my goodness!" she cried, putting the fish firmly back on the plate. "Oh my goodness! Look what I've done!" She put her hand to her mouth and began to laugh.

"What have you done?" I cried.

"Icing sugar," explained my mother, laughing. "With all the excitement, I rolled it in icing sugar."

Our eyes followed hers to the bag on the counter. She was right.

"Never mind," said my mother, brightly. "We'll give it to the cats. It'll be a real treat for them."

"We'll give it to Bogey," said Andrew, remembering his stinking boots and switching targets with impressive speed.

Bogey was sitting on the arm of his favorite chair, his claws tucked into his furry paw, poised to attack the next person who walked past.

Andrew hauled Bogey off the back of his chair and carried him into the kitchen.

My mother put the trout down on the floor.

Bogey didn't even bother to sniff it. One look was enough.

He turned in disgust and stalked out of the kitchen.

"Try Binker," suggested my mother, wanting to salvage something out of the situation.

Binker was Bogey's sister. She was gray with a white blaze on her face. Binker was my baby. I used to dress her up in doll's clothes and put her to bed in my doll's cot. *Tucked up tight.*

Even so she always managed to escape.

I found Binker. She was asleep in a patch of sunshine outside the back door.

Binker's response was different. She sniffed the trout twice and looked up in a puzzled sort of way and went back to where she had come from.

The trout was unceremoniously dumped in the garbage.

"Never mind," said my mother kindly. "There's lemon meringue pie for supper."

Later, my father came back from work and we told him the story of our fishing trip again and again. Or rather, Andrew did. He seemed to have taken over our adventure. It had suddenly become men's talk. And I was left out.

This was not the original idea at all. It was sup-posed to be the Adventure of the Fish Day. What's more, I was the one who had hauled it out of the river in the first place.

I glared at Andrew's pink excited face but said noth-ing. Then I remembered the lemon pie in the fridge. To soothe my hurt feelings, I sneaked into the kitchen and stole the thick curl of meringue in the middle.

After supper, Andrew and I watched Fred and Barney chuck boulders at each other in The Flintstones.

For once my mother didn't mind about the theft of the meringue curl on her pie. But Andrew did. He pinched me when he knew no one else was looking. Relations between us were rapidly cooling.

That night as I lay in bed, I heard my mother's voice on the telephone. "It was extraordinary. They managed it with a piece of string and a—"

There was a scream.

Andrew and I rushed out of our rooms. Halfway down the stairs, the receiver was dangling off the end of its cord and knocking against the wall.

My mother was crouched on the corner stair, looking up. At that moment, a bat swooped from its perch near the ceiling and flitted past us up the stairs.

"Bats!" I shrieked.

"Don't be dumb," said Andrew. "Bats can't hurt you." He patted my thick curly hair and smiled. "They only get caught in your hair."

I shrieked again.

"Andrew! Stop it!" ordered my mother. "Go to your rooms, both of you, and shut your doors." By now my father had appeared with a tennis racquet in one hand and a tea towel in the other.

"There's nothing to worry about," he said calmly. "It's only a bat. Shut your doors. We'll catch it and put it outside."

"But what happens if it's in *my* room?" I yowled.

"Pull your sheets over your head," replied my mother.

We ran upstairs. As I turned into my bedroom, Andrew leaned forward. "You know what bats do?"

"N-no."

"Bats dance on your sheets, Nancy," he said in a nasty singsong voice.

I stared at him wild-eyed. Then I slammed the door, jumped into bed, pulled the sheet over my head and lay trembling in the dark.

There was no sound except my own fast breathing. Then I heard it.

Scratch. Scratch. Scratch.

I twitched the sheet back a fraction. In the moon-light I could just make out the shapes in my room. A cupboard, a little dressing table, a chair, my dolls' house.

Scratch. Scratch. Scratch.

It was louder this time.

I pulled the sheet back a tiny bit more, easing the pillow on top of my head, just in case. Then I listened as hard as I could.

Scratch. Scratch. Scratch.

Rattle. Rattle. Thud.

My heart leapt in my throat. I thought I was going to choke.

The bat was trapped inside my dolls' house, barely a foot from my bed.

Who would save me from a fate worse than death?

I opened my mouth and screamed at the top of my voice.

In my mind, it was the bloodcurdling scream of the young girl in the white nightdress when Dracula appears at the end of her bed. In fact it was a hoarse squeak that somehow squeezed through the keyhole.

Miraculously the door opened and my mother appeared.

"What's the matter?"

"Mum!" I said in the huskiest voice I could manage. "Thank God you're alive!"

Four

The next day was Saturday. Andrew and my father had gone to watch the baseball game in Ottawa. My mother was moving furniture.

My mother was always moving furniture. This time it was the furniture in their bedroom. She was moving it back to where it had been the week before.

She was doing it for my father's sake, really. If he wanted to go to the bathroom in the middle of the night and the bed was in a new place, he never knew which direction to take. Sometimes he walked into walls. Sometimes he bumped into sliding glass doors.

Last night, after all the excitement of the bat and our extraordinary fishing trip, my mother had woken up to the sound of hangers clattering on the floor and someone thrashing around in the walk-in cupboard. "Elizabeth," a disembodied voice had muttered, "I don't want to alarm you but where the hell am I?"

"Bye, Mum," I shouted from the kitchen. "I'm going to Amy and Clare's house. I'm taking them on an expedition."

My mother appeared in the hall. She had a faraway

look in her eye and a lamp in one hand. She was rearranging furniture in her head. "Where to?"

"Oh, you know, some wild place infested with snakes." I paused and took a breath. "Oh, and thanks for rescuing me last night."

"That's OK." My mother laughed. Moving furniture always made her happy.

I pulled open the screen door and ran all the way up to the Linklaters'.

I loved going to Amy and Clare's house. Mrs. Linklater didn't seem to mind how much of a mess we made. Sometimes when we came back from the woods, we would rip off our muddy clothes and jump into their huge old bathtub which Mrs. Linklater let us fill right to the top with hot water. Then we slid up and down and made waves that splashed over the edge and soaked the floor.

The Linklaters' house had one big living room that was used for everything, and nothing was ever put away. Newspapers and magazines were piled under the chairs. The sofas were old and saggy and the curtains at the windows were faded by the sun.

Mrs. Linklater was an expert seamstress. She worked in one corner of the living room that looked as if it was decorated with material. Bits and pieces of fabric hung over the backs of chairs. Swatches were pinned to the wall.

There was only one rule in this house. No one was allowed to touch the sewing machine.

There wasn't a Mr. Linklater but there had been once because Mrs. Linklater wore a thick gold wedding ring.

Amy and Clare didn't talk about their father much. I don't think they ever knew him. They said he had been a brilliant young actor about to go to Hollywood when the Second World War happened. Then somehow, afterwards, he decided not to go to Hollywood and be a salesman instead. He died in a car crash near Sudbury. I once asked them what it was like not having a father. I couldn't even imagine my life without my father in the middle of it. But as soon as I had opened my mouth, I wished I had kept quiet. Usually Amy and Clare had something to say about everything. This time, they just looked away.

The Linklaters' house was rented, which meant to me that they were poorer than most of the other families I knew. The man who lived in it before had left a broken-down car called a Studebaker parked in the bushes. A Studebaker was one of my favorite cars. I loved the name and I loved the shape. It was huge and green with lots of chrome metal and a long curvy bonnet. Inside it was upholstered in cream leather with two big bench seats across the front and across the back.

If you couldn't find Amy and Clare at their house, they would always be in the back of the old Studebaker, wearing their hats and making up stories.

Clare's hat was a dented boater with a big black bow stuck on the back. Amy's was made of faded pink chiffon and had a tattered veil.

The hats had started after a royal visit to Ottawa. All the newspapers had pictures of the Queen sitting in the back of a fancy old car. She had been wearing a hat, of course.

So Amy and Clare decided that since they had a fancy old car, they would wear hats, too.

I checked the Studebaker first.

No hats.

I circled around the edge of the house. It was quiet except for the hum of a sewing machine. I peered in the window. Mrs. Linklater was bent over a length of material that lay in folds in her lap and flowed onto the floor. It was bright turquoise crisscrossed with thin scarlet and gold lines. It was the loveliest material I had ever seen.

I looked at Mrs. Linklater's face. Her eyes looked dreamy and faraway. For a moment something seemed strange but I couldn't think why. Then I realized what it was. It was as if she was smiling at a baby.

Mrs. Linklater looked up, feeling someone was watching her.

"Hi, Nancy," she said in her quiet voice. "I don't know where the girls are."

"Don't worry, Mrs. Linklater," I told her. "I'll find them."

She smiled. Her gray-blue eyes almost disappeared in a web of lines.

When I looked at Mrs. Linklater I always saw her as a young person grown old rather than just a grown-up. Her first name was Freya. It was a name I had never heard before. She said it was the name of a goddess and it came from a Viking myth.

I couldn't stop myself staring at the turquoise material. "That's beautiful material you're sewing, Mrs. Linklater."

"They're curtains for Mr. Chevrolet," said Mrs. Linklater, resting her hand on the cloth. "The fabric comes from London."

"It must have cost a lot," I blurted. Then I blushed because I knew it wasn't what I was supposed to say.

"I'm sure it cost plenty," said Mrs. Linklater with a smile. "I'll save you some scraps for your pictures if you like."

She knew about my pictures because I had given Amy one for Christmas. It was one of my best ones. It was a witch dressed in scarlet with pearl button eyes. She was dancing over mountains on black pipe-cleaner legs.

I looked at the turquoise cloth. It would be just right for a sea picture. I said thank you and ran across the scrubby yard that was in front of their house.

There was only one place left for Amy and Clare to be. Further into the woods was a meadow with an oak tree in the middle. About fifteen feet up from the ground was the perfect branch for a tire swing.

And there they were, sailing through the air, clinging on to the tire, whooping and screeching like two monkeys.

I switched into monkey and whooped to get their attention.

Amy beat her chest and howled back.

The tire slowly jerked to a stop. Amy jumped down. She had a thin pointed face with fine orange hair. Her eyes were the palest blue. The color was almost not there.

She waddled up to me and wrapped her arms around my chest like an orangutan.

"I'm a monkey," she hissed in my ear.

"I'm one of those upside-down things," said Clare.

"You mean a sloth," said Amy.

"Yeah," said Clare, hanging like a sloth from the tire.

"D'you wanna play jungle?" hooted Amy from somewhere near my armpit.

I switched out of monkey and eyed them both. "Nope," I said, firmly. "I'm leading an expedition."

I waited until I had their complete attention.

"An expedition into dangerous, wild country." I waited again. "Dangerous, wild country, *infested with snakes*."

Amy and Clare looked at each other. Clare dropped down from her tire.

Amy stood up and squared her shoulders.

"We'll come," they said.

We started to walk up to their house.

"Where to?"

"We cross the Yangtze and see how the raspberries are growing," I said. "Then, if we're still alive, we stop at Mr. Chevrolet's place and get some lemonade."

"The Yangtze!" cried Amy. "Yeah! Let's go to the Yangtze!"

The Yangtze was the name I had given to a squeaky, sagging wire fence. It was also the name of the biggest, wildest river in China, and China was one of the strangest, most exotic places I could imagine.

Crossing the Yangtze was the best bit of the journey to get to where the wild raspberries grew by the old railway tunnel. You held on and bounced up and down for as long as you liked. It was a really springy old fence so it made good bouncing. But best thing of all was the squeaky sound that filled your head and spread into the silent sunny woods around you.

Yang. Yang. Yang.

You could imagine you were anywhere. You could imagine you were crossing the Yangtze in faraway China.

Amy and Clare ran up the house and came back with a paper bag of oatmeal cookies.

We ate them as we walked through the woods.

"I saw Tracy Wilkins the other day," said Clare.

"So?" I said.

We munched our biscuits.

Clare looked like a little owl. She was tawny-eyed and olive-skinned.

"She was wrestling in the woods with Lawrence Murdoch," said Clare. She blinked. "And she was squealing like a stuck pig."

"Don't be dumb, Clare," said her sister. "They were kissing, not wrestling."

"Huh!" said Clare, not to be outdone. "It didn't look like kissing to me. And I bet her mother doesn't know."

I thought about Mrs. Wilkins's silvery little-girl's voice screeching down the telephone at my mother. If the facts of life weren't allowed in their house, real kissing wouldn't make it into the garage.

All of these things were more stubborn stains that

had to be scrubbed out so everything could look white and clean again.

I didn't like Mrs. Wilkins. She had a fixed sickly sweet smile but her eyes were hard and steely. She always acted as if someone important was watching her. Once I was there and she was ironing wearing high heels and lipstick.

My mother did the ironing in corduroy pants and an old checkered shirt of my father's. And if it was in the evenings she had a glass of ginger and rye sitting on the end of the board.

Sandra once told me her father had a more important job than my father. Which was easy enough because I had no idea what my father's job was anyway. All I knew was that he did something with the government and he didn't talk about it much.

When I told my mother, she just laughed and said Rick Wilkins was a sewage plant worker. I wasn't sure how important it was to be a sewage plant worker but I got the feeling it might not be as important as Sandra thought it was.

I knew the Wilkinses because they lived near and sometimes I played with Sandra. But Sandra was not allowed to play with Amy and Clare. When I asked Sandra why, Sandra had pulled a face as if there was a nasty smell under her nose.

"Mum says they're dirty. She says their house is a pigsty."

"It's not *dirty*," I had said angrily. "It's a bit messy, that's all."

"Same thing, Mum says. And Mum says Mrs. Linklater's wedding ring isn't gold."

This time I wasn't angry, just confused.

"What?"

Then Sandra explained how she had heard her parents talking about the Linklaters.

"For Chrissakes, Estelle," her father had said. "She wears a wedding ring, doesn't she?" But her mother had shrugged, then muttered, "Bet it's fake," and gone on ironing.

It took me a couple of minutes to understand. "You mean your mum thinks Amy and Clare's mum was never married?" I cried.

It was incredible. Everyone knew how Mr. Linklater had died.

But Sandra was getting bored. "I don't care, anyway." She wrinkled her pug-nosed dolly face. "Besides, Amy and Clare look funny."

I don't think I liked Sandra much. But there was something about her that I found irresistible. When her mother wasn't around, she smeared her lips with lipsticks called *Candy Kiss* and *Frosted Rose* and rubbed blue eyeshadow on the lids of her blank dolly eyes.

The thing with Sandra was you always got the feeling she was your friend until someone better showed up.

Anyway, she was right about Amy and Clare, they did look strange.

But I thought they looked strange and wonderful. They were like river nymphs or tree sprites, roaming in the woods and living in their make-believe worlds. They were the sort of kids who could have had wings tucked under their tattered blouses and nobody would be surprised.

I turned to Clare's little owl face.

"Did Tracy see you?" I asked.

Clare shook her head. "I was hiding inside a hollow log."

I didn't bother to ask her why. Clare spent most of her time up trees or inside them.

We walked on in silence. We were all thinking the same thing.

"Mrs. Wilkins would go crazy if she found out," said Amy, at last.

"I'll ask Sandra," I said. "I bet she'll know what Tracy's up to."

"I bet she won't," said Clare, blinking her tawny eyes. "I bet nobody knows but us."

Five

"How should I know?" said Sandra when I asked her if Tracy was going out with Lawrence Murdoch. "She never tells me anything."

A cunning look crossed her face. "But maybe now she'll have to." She squeezed my arm with her pudgy hand. "Thanks, Nancy."

My cheeks went hot. This wasn't what I had planned at all. "Promise you won't say anything," I said quickly.

Sandra smirked. "Maybe I will and maybe I won't."

"It doesn't matter anyway," I muttered, trying to cover my tracks.

"Yeah," replied Sandra.

She prodded the booklet that was lying between us. "Anyway, this is what we were talking about."

Sandra and I were sitting on her bed staring down at a black-and-white diagram of something that looked like the back half of a frog.

Flattened.

It came from a booklet Sandra had found in Tracy's room. On the cover, the booklet had a picture of two girls in flowery dressing gowns, sitting on a bed rather like we were. Both girls had perfect white teeth, rose pink lips and curling hair. One was a blonde. The other was a brunette. They both wore hairbands and were smiling.

The booklet was called *SPECIAL SECRETS*.

So far so good.

The problem lay with the flattened frog. Alongside its body was the word *uterus*. Beside its legs were the words *fallopian tubes*.

There were other words and other shapes, but Sandra wasn't going to be fooled. "I don't know about you," she said snootily, "but I don't have *that* inside *me*."

Sandra had got into a lot of trouble for giving me her fifteen cents for my version of the facts of life. Now she was determined to prove me wrong.

And since medical detail and funny names were not part of my repertoire, I was finding it difficult to defend myself.

I sighed understandingly. "I know it looks weird but everyone's got one of these inside." I tried to make her laugh. "Anyway, who cares? It's not as if we can see it."

"It's disgusting," said Sandra firmly.

"It's normal," I replied, using my best doctor's voice.

"Huh!" said Sandra, sneering. "You don't know what normal is."

"What do you mean?" I said. I could sense she had some trick up her sleeve.

"You never said anything about their clothes," declared Sandra triumphantly.

She flipped over a page. Now we were looking at a young mother with a baby in her arms. The baby was dressed in a knitted cardigan, lacy bonnet, frilly skirt and a pair of booties.

"What clothes?" I asked. "What are you talking about?"

"You don't know, do you?" sneered Sandra.

Despite every effort not to, I blushed.

"Ha!" crowed Sandra. "Exactly what I thought." She stared at me with her pudgy doll's eyes. "All babies are born with their clothes on."

"What?"

"So you don't have to go out and buy them," explained Sandra as if she was talking to a moron.

"That's crazy," I said. "Anyway, the clothes'd be all wet."

"Why should they?" demanded Sandra. "They'd be brand new, stupid."

"How do you know?" I asked quickly. I was trying to turn the tables on her.

Sandra waited for the last minute to deliver the final blow. "Mum told me," she said. She stood up as if the matter was closed. "Let's go watch TV."

"Sandra, honey," called a voice that was a mixture of Tinker Bell and razor blades, "is that you in there?"

Sandra stared at me, wild-eyed. The booklet lay open between us. "What am I going to do?"

"Hide it!"

With a bright red face, Sandra stuffed the booklet under her pillow just as the door opened and her mother stepped into the room.

Mrs. Wilkins took one look at me and one look at Sandra's red face and the smile on her perfect pink lips curdled.

"Hello, Nancy dear," she said. "I didn't think *you* would be here."

She turned her hard twinkling eyes on Sandra. "I want you to lay the table, honey."

"Do I have to?" whined Sandra. "Why can't Tracy do it?"

"I don't know where Tracy is," replied Mrs. Wilkins in an icy voice. She turned and smiled at me. "But of course, she knows she has to be home for supper."

It was my cue and I knew it.

Sandra wasn't listening.

"Can't Nancy stay the night?" she said. "We were going to watch TV. Then we were going to look through the new mail order catalog. I want—"

"No," snapped Mrs. Wilkins. She paused. "I mean, no, not tonight, sweetie. Nancy has to go home for supper."

"Why?"

I edged to the door. I knew Sandra's mother didn't like me but I don't think I realized until that moment how much she didn't like me.

I wanted to be out of that room as fast as possible. "Ah, because I have to," I muttered.

"What about tomorrow?" said Sandra.

"We're going shopping tomorrow," said Mrs. Wilkins quickly. "I'm taking you and Tracy to buy sandals."

Sandra's face lit up. In an instant, she forgot all about me. "What else?" she squealed. "Tracy got more than me last—"

"Thanks for having me, Mrs. Wilkins," I said. "Bye, Sandra."

"I want one of those blouses with pearl buttons," cried Sandra. "And a Glamour Girl vanity set."

"We'll see," replied her mother.

"What d'you mean, we'll see?" whined Sandra.

"I mean," said Mrs. Wilkins, "we'll see."

I shut the door and headed down the hall towards the kitchen.

In the kitchen was a round table with a flowery plastic cloth. Four purple raffia mats with fringes at the edges and a flower in the middle were set at perfect intervals. There was a knife, fork and spoon and a rolled pink and white checkered napkin at each place.

So much for Mrs. Wilkins wanting Sandra to lay the kitchen table.

Down the hall Mrs. Wilkins's voice had turned low and angry. "And just what do you think you're doing asking Nancy . . ."

There was a pause. "What's *this?*" shrieked Mrs. Wilkins. "What's *this,* Sandra Wilkins?" There was a *thwack* of rolled-up booklet on head.

Sandra began to howl. "It was Nancy—"

I shut the screen door as quietly as I could. Why didn't I listen to what my mother had told me time and time again? Sandra Wilkins was a low-down, lying little toad. And no matter how smart I thought I was, she would always get me into trouble.

My stomach turned over. And now I'd been dumb enough to tell her about Tracy and Lawrence Murdoch.

I made my way past the plastic fawn who stood

on the Wilkinses' front lawn staring down on the highway.

The fawn and I saw the car at the same time.

It was an old blue Ford and I knew it belonged to the Murdochs, who were friends of my parents and ran a gas station a few miles away.

The car pulled over out of sight of the Wilkinses' house. But from where I was standing, I could see Lawrence Murdoch behind the wheel and Tracy Wilkins sitting beside him.

Lawrence was seventeen and the Murdochs' only son. He was tall for his age with a heavy jaw and dark eyes. I watched as he leaned over to open Tracy's door.

Then my hand flew up to my mouth before I could stop it. They began kissing in a way I had never seen on TV. They were twisting and rolling all over the front seat.

A moment later Tracy jumped out of the car carrying a basket. She blew Lawrence a kiss and walked up the road to her house.

I don't know what I was expecting her to look like.

Maybe I thought she would look blurred and romantic, maybe confused, or maybe even agonized like the faces in the teenage magazines I'd looked through

in the supermarket. *Will he love me if I let him kiss me?*
Rules That Should Never Be Broken.

But there was no sign of anything like this on
Tracy's face. Quite the opposite, she looked really
pleased with herself.

I ducked behind some bushes as the front door
opened.

"Where have you been?" demanded Mrs. Wilkins.
Her face was hard and mean. The sweet smiling mask
had gone. "You should have been home hours ago."

Tracy lifted her basket. "I've been picking blueberries," she said in a voice as cold as her mother's.
"For your church picnic, remember?"

"Don't you talk to me like that, young lady,"
snapped Mrs. Wilkins. She stepped back into the
house.

"You were supposed to lay the table," squealed
Sandra from the doorway. "Mum's mad at you."

"Shut up, toad," said Tracy as she stepped onto the
porch.

"Tracy!" yelled Mrs. Wilkins. "Don't you dare talk
like that in my house."

Then something extraordinary happened. Tracy
lifted her basket of blueberries and tipped the whole
lot onto the grass.

I stared openmouthed because I saw from her face

as clearly as I saw the blueberries rolling down the perfectly mown lawn that Tracy hated her mother.

My stomach turned over. Hatred was something I knew nothing about. But that hard, cold look fascinated and horrified me.

At that moment, Mrs. Wilkins yanked open the door. I bent double and ran as fast as I could down to the highway.

Six

At the bottom of our road, I leant against a tree to get my breath back. In front of me our house was a friendly wooden face in the setting sun.

My father was mowing the grass. Andrew was kicking a football. My mother was brushing Sandy, our long-haired collie.

My heart stopped hammering. What was happening up at the Wilkinses' house had no place here.

A football whizzed past my ear.

"You wanna learn how to play?" shouted Andrew.

"You always get to catch," I shouted back.

"Aw, come on, Nancy," wheedled my brother. "There's lots of time before supper." He picked up the football and threw it in the air. "All you do is yell, 'Six, eight, seven, four, hike,' and throw the ball."

He bent over, held the ball between his legs, yelled "Six, eight, seven, four" and threw it at me.

Of course I missed it.

"Told you," said Andrew. "Why should I throw the ball to you if you can't catch?"

I stared at my brother's long, clever face and pushed the Wilkinses out of my mind.

"How can I learn if I never get any practice?" I answered. But even as I spoke, a plan was forming in my mind.

I picked up the ball and held on to it. "If I play football with you," I said slowly, "you have to play dolls' house with me after supper."

My plan was to have the dolls act out the scenes in the Wilkinses' house and see what Andrew made of it all. Even though he wasn't usually interested in what he called *boring girls' stuff*, what he thought might help me get a clearer grasp of what was going on up there. At any rate, I wanted to talk to somebody about it and Andrew was the first available person.

Andrew pulled at his hair and thought about my proposal. I knew he was trying to figure a way to worm out of his end of the deal.

At that moment our father walked past, dragging the old lawn mower. "Hi, Buttons," he said to me. "Where have you been?"

"Sandra's house."

"Oh."

My father was the original gentle giant. He was very tall, with blue eyes and gray hair. I don't ever remember it being any other color. He was slow-moving and quiet and always played fair.

I put my plan to him. He would be judge and jury if anything went wrong. "I play football with Andrew," I said. "Then he has to play dolls' house with me."

My father smiled at us and rubbed his mustache. "Sounds OK to me," he said.

I turned to Andrew. "Did you hear that?"

"I heard," replied Andrew.

My father turned and dragged the lawn mower towards the shed. "You kids sort it out," he called over his shoulder. "I'm going inside to sit down."

I've never known anyone to enjoy sitting down as much as my father. He would lower his long, skinny frame into a chair, settle himself down with his knees apart, light up a cigarette and sit. He could sit for hours as long as he had a newspaper, a cup of coffee and a packet of cigarettes.

I turned to Andrew. "So is it a deal or not?"

"It's a deal."

"Shake."

"Aw, Nancy."

"If it's a deal, shake."

We shook.

"OK," said Andrew. His eyes suddenly lit up. "This is what you do." He pointed to the other end of the lawn. "You stand there and throw the ball at me."

"Then what?"

"Then I kick it and you find it."

"Why can't I kick it?"

"Because you're no good at it."

I decided to let this pass since soon it would be my turn to call the shots.

For the next hour, I threw all kinds of balls. Some were high. Some were low. Some were just right and Andrew kicked them all over the place.

By the end even Andrew said I was getting pretty good at finding and throwing and we went in to have supper.

Supper was in front of the television that night. We watched I Love Lucy and ate homemade TV dinners.

My mother always bought frozen turkeys from the supermarket and made a huge mound of mashed potatoes and peas. With the leftovers, she made TV dinners. Sometimes I got the job of dishing out the portions of vegetables into their compartments in the silver foil trays while she sliced up the meat and poured over the gravy. Then the whole lot was wrapped in foil and stacked in the freezer.

I dumped my tray in the sink. Nothing was wasted in our house. The tray would be washed and used again.

"I'll just get things ready," I said in my airiest voice.

"What are you talking about?" muttered Andrew. He picked up a comic and pretended to read it.

"We're playing dolls' house," I said.

"You mean, *you're* playing dolls' house," he replied. "I'm reading *Dennis the Menace*."

"You promised."

Andrew shrugged. "So I broke my promise." He cracked the comic in his hands. "It happens all the time."

I turned to my father. "I played football before supper," I cried. "He promised to play dolls' house with me. You heard him."

My father looked up. He was sitting in his chair in the corner, knees apart, cigarette in one hand, newspaper by his elbow. "Andrew, go and play with your sister."

"I hate playing dolls' house," said Andrew.

"How do you know?" I countered. "You've never played before." A wild hope leapt in my chest. If I could just get Andrew to play once, he might get hooked forever.

My father picked up his newspaper again. "Too bad, kid," he said. "You made a promise. You have to keep it."

Andrew let the comic slide onto the floor.

I ran up the stairs, two at a time, went into my

bedroom and sat down cross-legged in front of my dolls' house.

It was an old-fashioned dolls' house. My mother had bought it secondhand when she was looking for old pine furniture It was painted pink and had a balcony held up by a balustrade of white wooden pillars. Most of the furniture had been sent from England where my grandmother lived.

Last Christmas, she had given me tables and chairs with beds and basins. There were boxes of knives and forks and candlesticks. There were lamps and chandeliers. And, of course, there were lots of tiny, exquisitely dressed dolls.

I loved my dolls' house and used to sit for hours in front of it making the dolls act out nail-biting dramas. My favorite books were the ones where dolls came to life.

Earlier in the summer I had tried to create the same effect with tree frogs. Every day I collected a dozen or so and every night I shut them in the dolls' house.

Then I lay in my bed, imagining them hopping from room to room. Soon they began to speak and shortly after, they turned into the dolls themselves, going about their business.

The only problem was that every morning, I had to pick up lots of dried-up, light-as-a-feather frog bodies.

Anyway.

I pulled open the double doors of the dolls' house and set out the dolls in their three-sided arena.

As I laid out the cars and the tricycles, I tried to imagine a scenario that Andrew would find irresistible. It had to have something to do with football or Disneyland. Andrew was obsessed with them both. Then I could ease in some of the things I had seen and heard at the Wilkins household. Of course I knew Mrs. Wilkins would have nothing in common with Lady Pimlico-Smythe, who was living in the dolls' house that week, but I thought I had worked a way round that problem.

The Wilkinses from Canada could be distant cousins of the Pimlico-Smythes. After all, I had enough dolls. The Wilkinses could arrive unexpectedly (having changed their clothes on the airplane) from a trip to Disneyland, bringing a football as a gift. Then things would go wrong with the Wilkins family . . .

I could hardly wait as I laid out the dolls.

What would Andrew think of a mother who told lies to her daughter to get rid of the friend she didn't like? What would he make of a daughter who hated her mother so much she did the worst thing she could think of to annoy her? I didn't have any blueberries but perhaps a tray full of glasses would do.

I could hear Andrew coming up the stairs. I tried

to ignore the fact that he was moving as slowly as possible.

At last he arrived at the door and slumped against the wall. "I'm here."

"Everything's ready," I gushed. "I thought of a really good story. It's all about this English family who discover they are crazy about football and—"

Andrew sat down beside me and picked up a doll.

I was amazed. I hadn't expected him to fall in with the spirit of things so quickly.

The doll he had chosen was the wrong one. Her name was Jessica and she never really did much. I picked up another to give him. "That's the wrong doll," I said. "This one's—"

"This is *my* doll," interrupted Andrew. He grasped it firmly round the waist as if it was a screwdriver. It was not the right way to hold a doll at all.

A clammy feeling fluttered across my stomach. Andrew was up to something. But I didn't know what.

"Look at this doll carefully," said my brother.

Again my hopes rose.

"Her name is Jessica," I began.

"Jessica is a naughty doll," said Andrew in his sing-song voice.

Then before I could stop him, he pushed Jessica like a broom through all the ground-floor rooms and knocked over the furniture.

I snatched the doll out of his hand. "You dirty rat!"
I shouted. "Get out of my room!"

Andrew got up. I had played right into his hands.
"You shouldn't shout," he said with a smirk.

And without another word he was gone.

For a moment I sat and stared at the dolls' house.
Rage and disappointment whirled around my head.

What use was a brother you couldn't talk to?
What use was a brother who never noticed anything
around him? Or who noticed things differently from
anyone else? And at a completely different speed.

Maybe that was it. Maybe I was going too fast. I
would just have to wait until Andrew got interested
enough. And even then, I knew there was always the
chance that he never would.

As I put back the cars and tricycles, the beds and
bureaus, even the tiny pitchers and washing bowls, I
tried to be philosophical about my defeat.

I remembered something that had happened at
Christmas when my grandmother had been staying.
The day after she had arrived, she had offered
Andrew and me double our week's pocket money to
tidy our rooms.

In those days, a week's pocket money was twenty-
five cents and we usually spent it on a bottle of pop
and a chocolate bar.

So fifty cents was a fortune. Not only did I tidy my

room, I polished my furniture, I dressed my dolls in new clothes. I even washed the sheets in my baby's cot because they were covered in Binker's fur.

When I told Andrew, he shrugged.

He had said no in the first place.

He liked his room as it was.

How could I have expected someone like that to be interested in what was happening at the Wilkinses' house?

I laid the doll called Jessica in her little bed and shut the double-fronted doors.

Somehow I would have to work out for myself what was really going on, and why.

Seven

Around the corner from our little inlet, the slow-moving water finally gave up and turned into a swamp. Here the water was brown and soupy and covered in green weed. We called this a lagoon. It sounded more exotic and jungly than swamp.

Andrew and I lay in the warm mud. It was soft, greasy mud, and it stank of rotten eggs. Behind us, under the trees, was a pail full of bullfrog tadpoles. We had managed to catch twenty of them. Now we were resting in the sun and I had just finished telling Andrew about Tracy and Lawrence and Tracy and her mother. It seemed a better sort of place than sitting in front of my dolls' house.

To my delight, he seemed mildly interested.

"'Bet Lawrence is planning to rob the store and drive out west," said Andrew. He was holding a stick and tracing the vague outline of a gun in the mud.

"Why would he do that?" I said.

"Get some money so he and Tracy can go to Disneyland," he replied, as if it was obvious.

I wasn't so sure. Not everyone was as obsessed with Disneyland as Andrew was.

"Who's going to Disneyland?" cried Amy.

It was amazing how Amy and Clare could walk through a wood without so much as a twig snapping.

"Lawrence and Tracy," said Andrew. "D'ya see our tadpoles?"

Clare nodded and sat down. "They stink when they die," she said.

"What do you mean, die?" I said, getting annoyed. I wasn't planning on letting these tadpoles die. I was going to train them to do tricks, so that by the time they grew into frogs, they would be able to perform a sort of hopping square dance. I'd buy a stripey tent, and people would line up to see them—

"We had some once," said Amy. "We did everything for them." She counted on her fingers all the good things her tadpoles had enjoyed. "We kept them in a big metal tub. We gave them stones so they could climb out of the water when they grew legs—"

"We even caught flies for them," said Clare. "They died anyway, and Ma couldn't use the tub anymore because it stank so much."

I slithered out of the mud and stared at the dark blobs waggling in the murky water. Each tadpole had a body the size of a plum. They were certainly moving much more slowly than when Andrew and I had first caught them. Perhaps they were starting to die already.

What with my failed dolls' house experiment, I was beginning to feel a bit guilty about my dealings with frogs. *The right thing to do* flashed up like neon lights in my mind. I picked up the pail and tipped it back into the lagoon.

Andrew barely noticed. He had a faraway look in his eyes and was drawing a picture of Mickey Mouse on the place where his gun had disappeared.

"What's this about Lawrence and Tracy going to Disneyland?" asked Amy.

Andrew sighed. "Some people get all the luck," he muttered.

I rolled my eyes and stared sideways at him. "We don't know for sure that's where they're going," I said.

Clare threw a stone in the thick green water. "So what do you know?"

I told them how I had seen Lawrence and Tracy kissing in Lawrence's car.

"Did they squeal like when they were wrestling?" asked Clare.

I shrugged. "I was too far away to hear."

For a moment nobody spoke. Andrew drew a big smile under Mickey Mouse's nose.

We watched the scum on the lagoon shimmer and shudder as water beetles skidded from plant to plant.

"I saw them this morning," said Amy, chewing on a long piece of grass. "They were in Lawrence's car again."

Amy put down her piece of grass.

Andrew and Clare sat up.

"Did you see Tracy's face?" I asked.

Amy nodded. "Yup. She looked like Cruella de Vil."

Andrew stood up. "I'm going swimming," he said. His eyes looked troubled.

"I don't understand it," he muttered.

I swung round and stared at him. At last I could share my worries. "Nor do I," I cried. "Tracy hates her mother. I saw it. It was like she was kissing Lawrence to spite her."

Andrew looked at me as if I'd gone mad.

"What are you talking about?" he said. He threw his stick into the pond. "I just never thought Tracy Wilkins would get to Disneyland before me."

As we stood up with him, I looked down in the mud. Mickey Mouse was vanishing fast.

Eight

An old wooden dock floated in the inlet. It had been built a few years back by a retired colonel. He had roped half a dozen heavy planks together and fitted them on top of six huge empty oil drums. A lump of cement at the end of a chain stopped the dock from drifting away.

We loved the dock. It could be anything. A desert island. A piece of the moon. A launchpad into the unknown.

We jumped into the water and swam over to it. We weren't supposed to swim on our own, but we always did. My mother had even stopped saying that if we drowned no one would find us in the murky water. There didn't seem any point anymore. As for Amy and Clare, they seemed as much a part of the river as a part of the woods. They swam like minnows. They jumped off the dock and set off to the other side of the narrow inlet where Andrew was paddling on his log.

Left on my own, I played my "prisoner escapes

from underwater prison" game. It was a cross between a thriller movie and my favorite TV show starring an underwater diver called Lloyd Bridges. It was also a good way to forget about the other problems that were on my mind.

I dived underneath the dock.

It was slimy and black under there. The hollow noise of the water trapped in the drums slapped at a different time from the river and made spooky booming sounds. I stared up at the ragged lines of sky showing between the planks. They looked like bars.

It was just how I imagined an underwater prison.

My heart began to pound. What would Lloyd Bridges do?

A second later, I prepared for my impossible escape. I counted slowly to ten. I took a deep breath—this one's for you, Lloyd!—then I sank into the muddy water.

I came up gasping and shouting. I'd made it! I was free! The sun was warm on my face. My eyes blinked in the unaccustomed bright light. In my mind's eye, Lloyd Bridges was watching me. He was proud and amazed.

He leaned over and whispered in my ear, *One day you're gonna be a great diver, Nancy.*

I clambered onto the dock and dried out in the sun.

Amy and Clare were sitting on the bank but there was no sign of Andrew.

"Where's Andrew?" I called.

"He's gone to Mr. Chevrolet's," shouted Clare as she squeezed out her orange hair.

I slid down off the dock and swam over to them. For a little while we sat together listening to the hot buzz of insects and watching the sunlight sparkle on the water.

Then Amy picked up a stick and snapped it.

"You know I said I saw Tracy and Lawrence." She sounded as if she had been bottling something up all afternoon.

"Yeah," I said.

"Well, I saw something else, too."

Clare and I pulled up our knees and waited.

"I was lying in the ambush place watching the cars go by," began Amy.

I knew the place Amy meant. There was a pile of big boulders by the side of the highway just opposite the slope leading up to the Wilkinses' house. One of the boulders was flat and hidden from the road by the others. Sometimes we used to lie there and throw pebbles at passing cars.

I flicked an ant that was crawling through the grass. "What did you see?"

Amy said that Mrs. Wilkins was on the front lawn polishing the fawn just as Lawrence stopped the car. Which meant, of course, she saw Tracy and Lawrence kissing in the front seat.

"Anyway," said Amy, "after Lawrence drove off, Mrs. Wilkins ran up to Tracy and shouted, 'You filthy slut! I never want to see that again.'"

Clare and I gasped. We had never heard this kind of talk before.

But there was more to come.

Amy took a deep breath. "Tracy yelled back, 'You're a slut, yourself!' Then"—Amy lowered her voice to a whisper—"Mrs. Wilkins slapped her right across the face."

My hands felt clammy even though the grass was warm. "Jeesuus!" I let the word escape from my lips like a slow hiss of steam. A *slut. Slut* was on the same page of my thesaurus as *prostitute*, which I had looked up only the other day in search of wider knowledge. *Slut* was beside *strumpet, trollop, wench, hussy*—and, finally, *bad woman.* Which was lucky for me since I didn't know any of the other words.

"What's a slut?" asked Clare.

I flicked another ant. "It means a bad woman."

Amy chewed on her piece of grass again. "I wonder why Tracy called her mother a, um, bad woman?"

We stared at the river.

"Maybe she is," I said. "Maybe that's why she goes to church so much."

"What d'ya mean?" asked Clare.

"To pay for her sins," I said.

"What sins?" asked Clare.

I shrugged. "How should I know?"

We stared at the river some more.

A story title from one of those teenage magazines flashed in front of me. *Her Guilty Secret.*

A cold feeling fluttered across my stomach. Maybe Mrs. Wilkins did have something to hide and whatever it was Tracy had found out about it.

I remembered Tracy's face as she dumped the blueberries on the lawn. Could Mrs. Wilkins's secret be the reason Tracy hated her so much?

"I don't like the Wilkinses," said Clare. "They're weird."

I got up. "Come on, let's go and get some lemonade from Mr. Chevrolet."

Mr. Chevrolet was sitting on his deck. "Ah! More explorers," he called down when he saw us. "Andrew and I have been waiting for you. The lemonade is ready."

Mr. Chevrolet made his lemonade with real lemons. He kept it in the kitchen in old pop bottles with corks banged in their tops.

Mr. Chevrolet was something different for each of us.

With Andrew he played chess and talked about ways of thinking about things. With me he talked about books. He gave me one of my most treasured possessions—a battered set of Arthur Mee's Children's Encyclopaedias. It didn't matter that it was old and most of the facts were out of date. I sat for hours reading amazing tales of skill and bravery and staring at diagrams of bubbles and air balloons and cross-sections of ocean liners built at the turn of the century.

With Amy Mr. Chevrolet talked about pictures and painters. And with Clare he talked about animals.

The three of us ran up the steps onto the shady wooden verandah. Mr. Chevrolet beamed at us all. But today he seemed to smile particularly at Amy and Clare. "Your mother has made me the most sumptuous curtains," he said. "My living room will become an Aladdin's cave."

"Ah, yeah," said Amy, smiling uncertainly. None of us had any idea what sumptuous meant. But Aladdin's Cave was a good place to be.

Mr. Chevrolet clapped his hands. "Nancy, come."

When it was time for lemonade one of us always went with him into the kitchen to carry the tray with the plastic tumblers. Today it was my turn.

We walked through the living room. It was a big room with a braided rug, comfortable chairs and a fire that he used in the winter. During the summer, a worn tapestry of hunting hounds stood in front of it. There were books everywhere. Some were on shelves. Others were in piles on the floor. The room had a deep easiness to it. It was the place where Mr. Chevrolet spent most of his time.

On the other side a corridor led to three bedrooms and a bathroom. At the back was a kitchen. It was a big house for one person.

We went into the kitchen. It was cool and shady. Thin blue and yellow curtains hung at the window. It was a tiny kitchen with a sink, a table and a couple of cupboards set into the wall.

As I took the tray from its slot under the sink, it occurred to me that Mr. Chevrolet might be able to help me understand what was happening at the Wilkinses' house.

"Why do some people pretend to be something that they're not?" I said.

Mr. Chevrolet reached into the cupboard and took down five tumblers. He didn't ask me why I had such a question. He just answered me.

"Perhaps because they're unhappy," he said. "Or perhaps they know they can never be what they want to be."

"But that doesn't mean they have to be nasty, does it?"

Mr. Chevrolet opened the fridge and took out a pitcher of lemonade. "No, it doesn't."

I put the tumblers on the tray. That was something else I didn't understand. How could Mrs. Wilkins be so nasty if she believed in God so much? God was supposed to be good. He was supposed to be an example for others to follow. At least that's what we were told at school.

"What does God say about people who are nasty and pretend to be something else?"

Mr. Chevrolet shut the fridge door. In the shadowy kitchen, I could feel his eyes watching me. Even if he did know who I was talking about, he didn't say. "God is our conscience, Nancy," he said. "Whether we listen to our conscience is up to us." He laid his hand on my head for a second. "And sometimes people don't listen."

He smiled at me and picked up the tray. "This is thirsty talk. Let's have some lemonade."

As we walked through his living room in the bright light, I noticed something lying on the table. It was a mask with a fierce red and orange face and a sharp-toothed, leering smile.

"Ah yes," said Mr. Chevrolet, following my gaze.

"I knew I had something to show you. It's from Mexico. Bring it out to the others."

It was a mask made by ripping wet paper into tiny pieces. Mr. Chevrolet called it *papier-mâché*. None of us had ever seen anything like it before. And as for Mexico, the only thing I knew came from a song called "Speedy Gonzales." Mexicans slapped mud on the walls of their *adobes*, ate *enchiladas* (whatever they were), and drank Coke which they kept in iceboxes.

Mr. Chevrolet put down the tray and held the mask in front of his face.

Immediately the person we knew disappeared and a thing with a leering smile took his place.

For a split second, it was as if we were seeing a part of him that he had hidden. A part of him that he pretended wasn't there.

I couldn't bear looking at it. "Take it off," I blurted. "Take it off. I hate it."

Mr. Chevrolet put the mask down. "It's not flattering, is it?" he said lightly. "Perhaps I should ask my friend to send me another one."

"No!" cried Amy. "I want you to stay just as you are!"

Mr. Chevrolet looked round at our unhappy faces. Then he looked at the leering mask. It was as if he was reading our minds.

He dragged over an old iron cooking pot. Then he struck a match, set fire to the mask and dropped it in the pot.

"Quite right," he said. "Things should be what they seem."

As he spoke he looked up at me. "And people should, too."

Nine

A few days later, I stood beside my mother in the kitchen and helped her make a spice cake.

Things had gone fairly quiet. The Linklaters were away visiting friends at Marionville, on the other side of Ottawa, and I had kept well clear of Sandra Wilkins.

I watched as my mother weighed a mound of raisins and dumped them into a mixing bowl. So far, I had cracked the eggs, weighed out the sugar and got the spices out of the cupboard.

I was trying to be helpful. What I really wanted was a fingerful of mix.

My mother bent down to get a roll of grease-proof paper from the cupboard under the sink.

My finger shot into the bowl, into my mouth and was back out again by the time she straightened up.

There is nothing like the taste of spice cake mix to encourage confidences. Perhaps it is the mixture of cinnamon and brown sugar. Or maybe it is the all-spice and the big fat raisins. Anyway, I suddenly wanted to talk.

The questions about Tracy and Lawrence had sparked off other questions. It was all to do with the front seats of cars and cupboards. Since cupboards were crucial in my scheme of things, what happened if they weren't in cars?

"If you kiss in a car, is it different?"

My mother sprinkled more cinnamon and half a teaspoon of nutmeg into the mixing bowl.

"Different from what?"

I squirmed. Why did she have to be so stupid? "Different from, you know, bedrooms and, um, stuff."

She picked up the beaters and plunged them into the bowl. "You can get pregnant in a car, if that's what you mean."

"But—" Then I stopped. What kind of car had cupboards?

She put down the beaters. Her green eyes bored into my brain. "What have you been watching?"

"Oh, nothing."

"You must have been watching something. What was it?"

It couldn't be a movie because she knew what we watched on TV. It wasn't a book because she knew what I had in my room and *The Famous Five* didn't go in for boys and girls grabbing each other in cars.

I knew I had one escape route. "Sandra had a magazine—"

"I might have guessed it was Sandra," said my mother, rolling her eyes. She picked up the cake pan and rubbed the inside with butter as if she was scouring a frying pan. "How Estelle can complain about you when her own daughters dress like jailbait, I have no idea."

"What's jailbait?"

In my mind's eye, I saw a huge stripey lollipop being dragged past a cell window on the end of a string. But I knew instinctively what she was talking about.

My mother violently disapproved of young girls wearing miniature versions of adult clothes. Especially anything with black in it. Worse was a pastel color with black. Worst of all was any outfit that included frilly, lacy or satiny bits.

It didn't matter that you could find them in the pages of the mail order clothes catalog. They were the sort of thing that Sandra and her sister might wear. But they might as well come from the moon as far as I was concerned. My clothes and indeed most of my mother's were made at home on her sewing machine.

The problem was that although I craved such garments desperately, my one and only experience with them had proved disastrous. Once at Ottawa's first big department store I had made such a fuss that my mother had given in and I was allowed to try on a couple of dresses I had chosen myself.

Andrew, my father and my mother sat while I dragged my prizes into the changing room with the saleslady, who had taken one look at my peeling red nose and scabby knees, and insisted on accompanying me. I was definitely the *I'm sorry I ripped it by accident* type.

My first choice was a shiny ("It's got nylon in it," sniffed my mother) green corduroy dress with a deep portrait collar in a different glossy black material. Various frilly fronts called *dickies* could be fastened inside the scooped neckline. A wide studded belt marked my nonexistent waistline.

The other had a full skirt, elbow-length sleeves and purple and red roses on a pale pink satiny background.

In the first one I looked like an Elizabethan retainer that had shrunk in the wash. In the second I looked like a bruised lobster.

Even my father, who tried to say kind things whatever the occasion, ran into trouble. "Very pretty, Buttons, but don't you think you look nicer the way you are?"

"You look dumb," was Andrew's response.

My mother had got up and helped me back into my own clothes.

"What's jailbait?" I asked again.

"Everyone knows *that*," announced Andrew, appearing at the back door. "It's what they call T-bone steaks in prison."

"It isn't."

"It is."

"It *iszunt*," I shouted. "Is it, Mum?"

"Let's take the dogs for a walk in Wakefield," replied my mother, undoing her apron and hanging it on the wall. "I think we could all do with some air."

"I'll get the leads," I said.

"No, I will," said Andrew quickly.

"Let Andrew get the leads," said my mother in an even voice.

Within seconds seven dogs were jumping up and down, barking.

My mother collected dogs. The newest arrival was a nervous mongrel puppy called Tinker.

On the whole, my father was philosophical about the dog members of our family. One would have been fine but seven was OK.

He was, however, experiencing teething difficulties with Tinker. My father always wore a hat driving. Twice Tinker had been sick down the back of his neck and knocked over his hat so he couldn't see where he was going.

So it came as no surprise that my father declined the prospect of a walk in Wakefield. He was sitting in the living room, listening to a baseball game on the radio, nursing a cup of coffee and smoking a cigarette. He lifted his hand off the arm of his chair. "Bye, bye."

We piled into the car. The dogs barked hysterically and jumped from front to back. It was always the same until my mother pulled onto the highway and bellowed, "Settle down!" Then they took their places and waited, eyes sparkling, tails flopping, tongues panting.

We drove along the road to Wakefield. Wakefield was a small town right on the Gatineau River. If you put your hand out of the car window, you could almost trail your fingers in the water.

The biggest building in Wakefield was the cottage hospital. It was a friendly white and green building with lawns and bright sunny flowerbeds.

A wooden bridge with a pitched roof crossed the river. Over the other side were the wooded hills known as Wakefield Heights.

We only ever came to Wakefield for one of two reasons: to walk the dogs or see the doctor.

My mother slowed down as we headed towards the white-painted covered bridge.

In my mind's eye, we were crossing the bridge. The car wheels were rattling over the wooden boards. I went through my usual scenario. You could see daylight through those boards. What if they gave way and we plunged into the river? There was only one thing to do.

(Lloyd Bridges would have done the same.) I rested my hand on the window winder. If I didn't lose my nerve there would be just enough time to wind down the window before we hit the water. . . .

A car was parked on the side of the road in front of us. It was sparkling white with a shiny chrome grille that glittered in the sun like polished sharks' teeth. Only one family had a car as clean as that.

The Wilkinses.

Mr. Wilkins was getting into the driver's seat. His face looked red and lumpy, like a pile of stewing steak. In the backseat Tracy was glaring fixedly out of the window towards the river. Beside her, Sandra sucked on a lollipop. When she saw me, she stuck her tongue out and licked her lollipop more slowly.

At that moment, Mrs. Wilkins swung round, whacked Sandra on the side of the head and threw the lollipop out of the window.

Then they pulled on to the road and drove off.

We turned into the darkness of the bridge.

"Tracy Wilkins and Lawrence Murdoch are going to rob the gas station and drive out to Disneyland," said Andrew as if this sort of thing happened all the time.

He was sitting in the front so I couldn't see his face.

"What on earth are you talking about, Andrew?"

replied my mother. But I could tell from her voice that she was slightly unnerved by what she had seen.

By now we were over the bridge and driving along the dirt track towards the place we usually left the car.

It was my turn. Somehow it didn't come out right. "Tracy and Mrs. Wilkins are sluts."

My mother pulled off the road and slammed on the brakes. Half the dogs fell onto the floor. They clambered back up onto the seats and began to bark. They knew it wasn't our usual place but it was good enough for them.

"Shaddup!" bellowed my mother in true Flintstone style.

They did.

We got out of the car in a flurry of dancing dogs.

My mother grabbed a handful of leads and we started walking. "So," she said, fixing us both with her warrior's eye. "Just what's all this about?"

Ten

A couple of days later Andrew and I were sitting outside eating peanut butter and jelly sandwiches and chunks of watermelon.

"Oh my God," said Andrew in a low voice. "Look who's coming."

I looked up.

Sandra Wilkins was skipping down the road towards us.

"What's Mum gonna say?" muttered Andrew.

I shrugged. Our mother had made it very clear in Wakefield what she thought of Tracy and Sandra. Tracy was a jumped-up little madam who would come to no good and Sandra was a troublemaker and a liar. And as for Mrs. Wilkins, if she had a guilty secret, it was none of our business.

"Hi, Nancy, hi, Andrew," said Sandra, sitting down beside us and picking up a sandwich. "Mum's cleaning house so I've come to play with you."

She sounded as if she was doing us a favor.

"Does your mother know you're here?" I said.

Sandra stuffed another sandwich into her mouth. "Nope."

Andrew picked up his plate and passed it to my mother through the kitchen window. "Sandra's here."

"I know," said my mother.

I could tell from the sound of her voice and the crash of cutlery in the kitchen that she was definitely not happy with the news.

As Andrew passed my chair, he leaned down and hissed in my ear, "Get rid of her."

I glared at him. How was I supposed to do that? I said the first thing that came into my head. It was what I always said when a fast getaway was called for.

"Do you wanna go on an adventure? I know a great place called the Yangtze. . . ."

Sandra looked over her shoulder to where Andrew was now standing. "I'm not going on no dumb nature trails."

She leaned forward. "I've got a *real* plan."

Andrew stuffed the last piece of watermelon in his mouth. "I'm going to see if Mr. Chevrolet's in," he said. He stared hard at me. "Don't come." Then he turned on his heel and walked off.

Even though Sandra had never been to Mr. Chevrolet's house, I didn't argue. Something told me that Mr. Chevrolet wouldn't like Sandra any more than Andrew did.

As soon as Andrew was gone, Sandra grabbed my hand. "You gotta come with me," she breathed wetly in my ear. "You're my best friend."

"Where?"

"You'll see. We're going to play detectives." She pulled me up. "An' if you tell anyone, worms will eat your brains."

I promised my mother we were going blueberry-picking.

As I followed Sandra back up the road, she told me that the day they went to Wakefield, Tracy and her mother had gone off together and her father had bought her a lollipop.

When they all met up again, everyone was in a bad mood and there was a funny medicine cabinet smell in the car. Sandra said the only time she had smelt a smell like it was at the hospital. But when she asked her mother if she'd been there, her mother told her to shut up and mind her own business.

"I saw what happened next," I said.

"Oh yeah. You did."

We crossed over the highway and I followed Sandra through the woods and down to the back of her house.

I watched in amazement as she removed the outside screen that covered the ventilation shaft under the house. All houses around us had a space between the ground they were built on and the ground floor. Only that summer my mother and I had slithered on our backs underneath our house to stuff wads of prickly insulation between the joists that held up the floorboards. It was a horribly hot sticky job but when the winter came, we would be glad we had done it.

"What are you doing?" I said as Sandra quietly laid the screen up against the wall.

"I told you," replied Sandra with a sly look on her pudgy face. "We're going to play detectives."

She rested the screen against the wall and we crawled underneath the house. For five minutes we lay in the sweaty gloom looking up at wooden floor joists and listening to the even drone of a vacuum cleaner.

The Wilkinses hadn't insulated their house so you could hear everything as if it was happening in the room next door.

"This is stupid," I whispered, trying not to breathe too loud.

"No, it's not," hissed Sandra. "Mum and Tracy were up to something in Wakefield and I wanna find out what."

"You're crazy," I said. "You're not going to find out anything hiding here."

"How else am I going to find out?" muttered Sandra sulkily. "I tried asking Tracy and she hit me."

"What if we get caught?"

"We both get into trouble," replied Sandra.

Then I understood why I was there. We would both get into trouble but I would get the blame. My mother was right: Sandra was a liar and a trouble-maker. I decided to get out as fast as possible.

At that moment the telephone began to ring.

"Shh!" hissed Sandra. "Stop moving!"

The noise of the vacuum cleaner stopped. Foot-steps creaked above our heads.

"Hello." Mrs. Wilkins's voice was high and edgy. "Oh, hi, Cathy. Yeah, I'm doing a little cleaning. Yeah, Rick's trying to talk some sense into her. You saw what?" There was a pause.

"Who's Cathy?" I whispered to Sandra.

"My aunt," hissed Sandra.

The voice changed. "At eight in the morning com-ing out of the Riverview Motel? You sure it was Freya Linklater? I thought they were visiting friends in Marionville." She laughed in a nasty way. "Well, I guess the kids were in Marionville. What did he look like?"

Again the nasty laugh. "Yeah, I know him. He's the Polish guy that lives around here."

My face went hot and red. Mrs. Wilkins was talking about Mr. Chevrolet.

What was wrong with Mrs. Linklater and Mr. Chevrolet being at the Riverview?

I nudged Sandra.

"Shaddup!" hissed Sandra. "Mrs. Linklater, eh?" I could hear a smirk spreading across her face. "I knew we'd hear something juicy."

"What do you mean, *juicy*?" I croaked.

"Don't be stupid, Nancy. It was you that told me what people do in cupboards. And every motel bedroom has a cupboard, you know."

"What are you talking about?"

"You don't really know anything, do you?" sneered Sandra.

She began to talk as if I was a moron. "Mum thinks Mrs. Linklater and that Polish guy were making babies in the Riverview Motel."

My stomach turned over. I thought I was going to be sick. *Mrs. Linklater and Mr. Chevrolet making babies?* How could Mrs. Wilkins think *that*? Mrs. Linklater and Mr. Chevrolet hardly knew each other. Anyway, Amy and Clare would have been with them somewhere. Mrs. Linklater would never have left them behind.

I stared at Sandra's white, fat face. I couldn't see

her eyes but I could imagine them glittering. How could she believe babies were born with clothes on and yet be such a dirty, suspicious little brat?

"I'm going," I mumbled.

I slithered over to the other side of the house and the ventilation hole.

There was a crunch of car tires on the drive. A shiny silver hubcap stopped in front of my face. It was Mr. Wilkins and Tracy.

"Now get this straight," began Mr. Wilkins. He sounded like he was trying not to lose his temper.

I wanted to close my ears but I couldn't. It was like being trapped in some horrible nightmare.

"We have to talk to your mother," said Mr. Wilkins. "Then we can decide."

Tracy's voice was brittle. "I don't see why you're both making such a stink."

When she spoke again, her voice was hard and triumphant. "It's not as if it hasn't happened before."

"What are you talking about?" snapped Mr. Wilkins.

There was silence for a moment. Then Tracy began to scream. It was a harsh, shrill sound. "You can keep your lousy morals, Dad. I've seen my birth certificate. I've seen your marriage certificate. It takes nine months to make a baby. Mum was pregnant with me when you got married!" A car door slammed. "So leave me and Lawrence alone. We want our baby and I want out of this hellhole."

"Tracy! Come here!"

There was a patter of shoes up the outside stairs. A screen door banged.

"Don't you dare upset your mother!" roared Mr. Wilkins.

I lay in the dark, my heart pounding. So that was it. Tracy Wilkins was going to have Lawrence Murdoch's baby. That was why they had gone to Wakefield. Mrs. Wilkins had taken her to see the doctor.

The car door slammed. I rolled as far away from the ventilation hole as I could without making a noise. The next minute, I saw Mr. Wilkins's legs in the sunlight.

The legs turned into the dark shape of his body as he bent down.

My insides turned to jelly. If he stuck his head inside and looked around, he'd see me.

I saw him move and heard the scrape of the screen as he picked it up and began to fit it in place. "Bloody kids," he muttered.

"Rick!" shouted Mrs. Wilkins. "Rick! Where are you?"

"I'm down here," yelled Mr. Wilkins. "Some bloody kid musta—"

"I don't care about some bloody kid, " yelled Mrs. Wilkins. "Get your ass up here, now!"

I watched in slow motion as Mr. Wilkins hesitated.

"Rick!"

The screen moved to one side. He stood up and his two legs were two dark poles in the square of light.

A second later, there was the heavy tread of his feet on the outdoor steps.

"What did Tracy say?" whispered Sandra, crawling towards me.

"Find out for yourself!" I croaked.

I squeezed out through the empty window and crouched like an animal in the shadow of the house. It took a second for my eyes to get used to the light. From inside the house I could hear Mr. and Mrs. Wilkins shouting Tracy's name. There was the sound of someone banging on a door.

I skirted round to the front of the house and ran across the lawn. The blank-eyed fawn was still staring down onto the highway.

I thought about some of the things Tracy had said. *Leave me and Lawrence alone. I want out of this hellhole.*

I tried to imagine hating your family so much you'd want to run away from them. It seemed impossible. Besides, even if you wanted to, you couldn't. Your parents would stop you.

So maybe that's where having a baby came in. It suddenly made you grown up and you could do what you liked. You could leave your family and no one could stop you.

I thought of Tracy's hard, triumphant face as she walked away from Lawrence Murdoch's car.

Suddenly I realized that having a baby was exactly what she had planned.

As I crossed the highway, I looked back up at the Wilkinses' house. It was so white and so neat. You would never guess all the bad things people did and said inside it.

I could feel my face flush and my throat get tighter and tighter.

The Wilkinses' house should be painted black. It should be surrounded with piles of stinking garbage. DANGER. KEEP OFF signs should be stuck into the perfectly mown lawn.

Tears began to prick at my eyes.

I didn't care about Tracy.

But I did care about Mrs. Linklater and Mr. Chevrolet. And I hated Mrs. Wilkins making them dirty with her own sick, nasty suspicions.

Eleven

Andrew was coming up the road as I ran down it. He took one look at my face and knew something had happened.

"Don't go home," he said, tugging my arm.

"Why?"

"I've got something to show you."

I sniffed. "What?"

"I've found a cave."

"Where?"

Andrew smiled like a cat. "Do you wanna trade secrets?"

"How do you know I've got a secret to trade?" I muttered, knowing it was hopeless to pretend I didn't.

Andrew patted me on the shoulder and danced from foot to foot. "Do you wanna trade, or not?"

It was a familiar routine, and it made me feel better.

"Maybe," I said.

"Follow me, then."

We were heading down to the river.

"Was Mr. Chevrolet at his house?" I asked, as casually as I could manage.

"Yup," said Andrew. "But we didn't play chess be-cause he was painting his bedrooms." He paused. "He let me choose the color for one of them."

I couldn't think why Mr. Chevrolet would bother to paint his bedrooms. It wasn't as if he ever used them except for stacking books in. And as for asking Andrew to choose a color, Andrew was completely color-blind. "What color did you choose?"

"Yellow," said Andrew, in a definite voice. "But-tercup yellow."

He looked sideways at me. "What happened at Sandra's house?"

So I told him and I told him about Mrs. Wilkins's nasty laugh and what Sandra had said about Mrs. Linklater and Mr. Chevrolet.

"Huh!" said Andrew. "The Riverview garage is just behind the motel. The Linklaters' car must have broken down."

A huge sense of relief washed over me. But I had to be sure. "How do you know there's a garage?"

"Dad and I got gas there once," replied Andrew. "And the place was full of cars being fixed."

"Then why didn't Mrs. Wilkins think of that?"

Andrew took a deep breath as if he was going to say something he'd never said before. "Because she's a dumb bitch," he said. "And Sandra's a sickbrain."

For a second, we were silent. Then I let out a whoop of joy.

"Mrs. Wilkins's a dumb bitch!" I shouted at the top of my voice. "Mrs. Wilkins's a dumb bitch! Mrs. Wilkins's a dumb bitch and Sandra's a sickbrain, too!"

By this time we had reached the railway tracks.

Andrew looked sideways at me. "Is that your whole secret?"

"Half of it."

"OK."

Instead of crossing the tracks down to the river, Andrew turned left. At that moment, one of our dogs, called Daisy, appeared from the bushes. She was panting and her feathery tail wagged back and forth. She must have run all the way from the house.

I picked her up and hugged her. But Daisy didn't like being hugged. She wriggled out of my arms and bounced up and down on the tracks.

"We'll have to take her," I said.

"That's all right," said Andrew generously. "She can protect us against trolls."

"What?"

"Things that live in caves, dummy."

We walked down the tracks past the pond where the giant bulrushes grew. I looked beyond the pond to the strip of bright green meadow that sloped down to the river. It was hot and everything seemed to sizzle.

After the darkness and the nastiness at the Wilkinses' house, it was good to be here.

Suddenly all the relief disappeared and a tear dribbled down my cheek.

Andrew cocked his head and looked at me like a curious bird. "It's only a secret," he said. "All you have to do is tell me."

A roar filled my head and my face went scarlet. "You weren't there," I sobbed. "It was horrible. It was—"

At that moment we heard the train toot. Then it was coming round the corner and heading straight for us.

It was what we had been waiting for for years. We would jump clear with seconds to spare . . .

Neither of us moved.

The train tooted again.

We still didn't move.

Then Daisy barked.

My mother had always told us that if we heard a train coming, we had to grab the dogs so we were all standing on the same side of the tracks. That way no dog would try to make a last-minute attempt to cross.

I grabbed Daisy and Andrew grabbed me. We jumped off the tracks and rolled down a thorny bank into a ditch. A second later the engine roared past, a big iron cow-pusher splayed out in front. The train was huge and black and incredibly noisy.

Wagon after wagon rattled past. It seemed to go on forever. Then it was gone as suddenly as it had come.

"Jesus Christ!" whispered Andrew, pulling a bramble out of his hair. "That was a close one."

Daisy squirmed out of my arms and began yapping.

We climbed back up the bank and onto the tracks. Our arms and legs were scratched with bramble cuts.

Andrew put his ear to the rail just like they do in cowboy movies. "It's far away now," he said in his deepest voice. "So what's your secret?"

The fright of the train made me feel silly and light-headed. I wanted to tell him, but I couldn't. Instead I danced up and down.

"Where's your cave?" I shrieked. "I bet you haven't found one."

"Of course I have," shouted Andrew.

We ran on and off the rails along the tracks. Half a mile up, he pointed beyond a clump of trees to a stony outcrop on the side of a field. "It's over there."

Once again we scrambled down the bank, through the trees and up the other side.

A scrubby field seemed a strange place for a cave but Andrew seemed to know exactly where he was going. At last we came to large flattish stone that lay on its side against a big granite boulder. Between the two was a tuft of rough grass. Daisy took one look, pushed through the tuft of grass and disappeared.

"It's down there," said Andrew. "You have to sort of drop into it."

For the second time that day, I wriggled into a dark space. I stuck my legs in first and lowered my-self down.

"Are you sure it's a cave?" I said. "It's more like a hole."

"Wait till you get down a bit more," said Andrew.

As he spoke, I could suddenly swing my legs in the air. I found holds for my feet and let myself down.

"Here," said Andrew. "Take this and don't drop it." It was his precious metal flashlight.

He let himself down beside me. Then he took the flashlight and flashed the beam around us. We were in a big four-sided cavern. It must have been about twenty feet square. The ground was dry and sandy and covered in leaves. On one side there was a rough arch. We crept over to the arch and shone the light through it. There was another cavern only this one was smaller.

Daisy began barking in the smaller cavern. She sounded muffled and ghostly.

I thought of the cave in The Swiss Family Robinson.

How they had furnished it from the wrecked ship, hung carpets on the walls, rigged up bunks and cooking stoves. "We could live here," I whispered. "All it needs is a few sheets and some cardboard boxes."

Even Andrew was pleased. "Pretty good, isn't it?" he said. "I found it, remember."

I was too excited to argue with him, even though I had known the minute Daisy pushed through the tuft of grass that she had been the one who had found it, not Andrew.

We sat down on the ground and leaned against the stone walls. In my mind, I was lowering down supplies, arranging things in their right place. Preparing for the first meal.

"So tell me the other half of your secret," said Andrew.

I told him. When I had finished, we drew in the sand with sticks for a bit. Then Andrew said, "So do you think Tracy will still go to Disneyland or not?"

"Andrew." I took a deep breath. "I told you. She's going to have a baby. Lawrence's baby."

"That's crazy," said Andrew. "Who wants a baby?"

I shrugged. "I think Tracy does even if Mr. and Mrs. Wilkins don't." I drew a stick man with a large stomach holding hands with another stick man. "I think she wants to marry Lawrence to get away from here."

"Huh!" said Andrew. "Lawrence won't want to

take her. I mean, you can't have fun in Disneyland with a baby."

"Andrew," I said again. "A baby takes nine months to grow. Anyway, will you stop talking about Disneyland? Nobody said they were going there in the first place."

"They'd be crazy not to," insisted Andrew stubbornly. "Especially if they get enough money out of the gas station."

He drew a picture of a six-shooter in the ground. "I'd go if I were them." He paused and added forlornly, "Baby or no baby."

At that moment, Daisy's muffled barking turned into shrill yelping.

We jumped up and shone the torch through the arch. In the corner was a mound of bristling grayish-white quills. Beside it stood Daisy, squealing and pawing at her bloody nose.

"Jesus Christ!" shouted Andrew. "It's a porcupine!"

Until then we had been speaking quietly. Now Andrew's words crashed around our heads like fireworks. I thought of rock falls and avalanches. One more loud noise and we could be trapped here forever. We would die of thirst and hunger. They would find our skeletons lying in the sand, just like those skeletons they found when they dug up the treasure in *Treasure Island*. . . .

"For Chrissakes, Andrew, shut up!" I whistled for Daisy. "Let's get out of here."

Andrew scrambled up first. I passed him the dog and climbed out myself.

We stood in the late afternoon sun and brushed the grit from our hair and clothes. We were both so disappointed, neither of us spoke. We had been looking for a cave for ages.

"It's no good if there's a porcupine there," said Andrew at last.

"No."

We started to walk up the ridge.

"I was going to call it the *rendezvous*."

"What's that?"

"It's French for 'meeting place,' dummy," muttered Andrew in a miserable voice.

"Oh."

"But it's no good if there's a porcupine there."

"No."

We reached the highway and set off towards home. I let Andrew walk in front and I lagged behind. It seemed as if everything around me was going wrong.

Twelve

"The Linklaters are back," said my mother the next morning after breakfast.

"How do you know?" I asked.

"I saw their car outside when I took the garbage to the dump," said my mother. "If you want to go up there, tidy your room first."

"OK."

We didn't bother to say hello even though we hadn't seen each other for two weeks. I stood in the doorway of Amy and Clare's bedroom getting my breath back. I had run all the way to their house as soon as I'd tidied my room.

Amy and Clare's bedroom looked as if a tornado had rushed in the door, done a few turns and rushed out again. It was one of those resident tornadoes because each time I came their room was in a different kind of mess. This time, they had upended their bedsteads and draped them with blankets to make a shelter. Their mattresses were on the floor underneath. In the corner a stack of chairs reached drunkenly up to the ceiling. The tornado must have missed them.

They had been there since a Jack and the Beanstalk game we had played a few weeks back.

Amy did a pirouette and stopped, one foot pointing in front of the other. "So what do you think of my haircut?" she said. "I did it myself."

She peered at herself in a small vanity mirror. "It's supposed to be like Peter Pan's."

Her fine orange hair looked as if it had been chewed by rats.

"Mine's supposed to be an upside-down bowl," said Clare in her deep voice. "I put a bowl on my head and cut round it."

Clare's hair looked like a cropped horse's tail. It was short and thick and stuck out at the back.

I didn't know what to say.

"What did your mother think?"

Amy threw back her head in a jaunty Peter Pannish sort of way. "Oh, she didn't mind. She went away for a week and when she came back she had a new haircut."

"Mrs. Somers was *fuurrrious* when we cut ours," said Clare. She rolled the word like a candy round her mouth.

"Who's Mrs. Somers?"

"She's the lady we were staying with in Marionville," said Amy. "She's English." She laughed. "She said we were *impossible*."

"Absolutely *impossible*," shrieked Clare, doing her imitation of the Queen. "But the farm was great."

"You stayed on a farm?" My eyes lit up.

It was my dream to have a farm. There would be lots of big red and white barns. Chickens would wander in the yard. Cart horses would pull wagons full of hay. There would be pitchforks and and scare-crows and a crazy-eyed billy goat who really did eat tin cans. . . .

"What did you do?"

Amy shrugged, slowly. She knew I was hanging on every word. "Oh, you know, farm stuff."

"What do you mean, farm stuff?" I almost shouted.

"I rode a cart horse," said Clare. "And I milked a cow." She giggled. "And I squirted Amy in the face."

"It was *hot*," shouted Amy, pretending to wipe milk from her eye and lick her fingers.

I was beside myself. I'd never ever tasted milk fresh from a cow.

"What else did you do?" I asked in a choked voice.

"I got given a calf," said Amy. "But it butted me." She pulled back her lips and wiggled her front tooth. "So they gave me a piglet instead."

I couldn't believe my ears. "You mean just like Wilbur in *Charlotte's Web*?" I gasped. I looked around for a piglet nestling in a box of hay. The room was such a mess it would be easy to miss it. "Did you keep it?"

If Amy and Clare had a piglet then maybe I could have one. It could live in the meadow down by the swings. I'd build it a house. I'd feed it scraps and call it Marvin. . . .

"Nope." Amy shook her head. "We were going to, but Mum said it wouldn't like being in the car for such a long time."

Of course their car had broken down. I'd forgotten about that. Mrs. Linklater was right. A piglet could get very unhappy hanging around a garage.

"What happened when your car broke down?" I asked. "Andrew said he's been to the Riverview garage with Dad."

"Our car never broke down." Amy stared at me.

"Where's the Riverview garage?" said Clare, looking puzzled.

I began to go red. "Sandra Wilkins said—I mean Andrew said—" I stared at the floor. "Shame about the pig, though," I muttered, trying to change the subject.

It didn't work.

"Sandra Wilkins?" repeated Amy, angrily. "What would Sandra Wilkins know about us? We never see Sandra Wilkins. What was she doing talking about us, anyway?"

"We don't like Sandra Wilkins," said Clare.

I was going hot and prickly and redder and redder. Andrew had been so sure that the Linklaters' car had broken down. In turn, I was sure that he was right. That was the reason for Mrs. Linklater to be outside the motel with Mr. Chevrolet.

They'd gone over for a cup of coffee while the brakes were being mended.

Oh, shut up! I told myself. You're making it up. You don't know *anything*.

In my mind, I heard Mrs. Wilkins's nasty laugh. *The kids were in Marionville, anyway.*

I heard Sandra's gleeful voice. *I knew we'd hear something juicy.*

Suddenly, I felt sick to my stomach. "I hate Sandra Wilkins, too," I said furiously. "I never want to see her again, ever."

At that moment, Mrs. Linklater appeared at the door. She was holding a brown paper bag. "Your sandwiches are ready, girls." She watched me curiously. "Are you feeling all right, Nancy?"

I looked up at her. There was something different about Mrs. Linklater. Now that I saw it I wondered why I hadn't noticed it the moment I had come into the kitchen. She looked younger. The lines on either side of her mouth had almost disappeared. Her new short hair suited her and she was wearing pearl ear-rings. She never used to wear earrings. Maybe they were new, too. Maybe she had got them when she was away.

"Sandra Wilkins told Nancy our car broke down," said Amy.

I felt dizzy like I was teetering on the edge of a cliff. Would they mention the Riverview? What would I say?

Mrs. Linklater looked around at all three of us.

"Sandra Wilkins is always telling somebody something," she said lightly. "And it's usually something they don't need to know."

She smiled at me and patted me on the head. "The girls say you're taking them on an adventure. Where are you going?"

"We're crossing the Yangtze," shouted Clare.

"It's our favorite place," cried Amy. "And we haven't been there for *two weeks!*"

She put her hands on my shoulders and jumped up and down.

Suddenly it was like old times again. I felt as if I'd stepped back from the cliff. Everything would be all right now.

Clare took the paper bag from her mother's hands and skipped into the kitchen towards the door.

"And we're going to pick raspberries," said Amy.

"That's sounds fun," said Mrs. Linklater. "How about some cartons to put them in?"

We followed Clare into the kitchen.

I watched as Mrs. Linklater reached above the sink to a broken wooden drainer stacked with old cartons. Then my eyes slid sideways past the drainer to a cluttered mantelpiece over an empty fireplace. On top of the mantelpiece was a box of cigarettes. Propped up beside them was a packet of matches. *Riverview Motel* was written across the front.

I blinked and looked again. Then I quickly looked away. A cold fizzy roar filled my head. It was like being in the middle of a snowstorm and realizing you have no idea where you are.

"Nancy." Mrs. Linklater's voice seemed to come from miles away. "Nancy."

She was holding out an old milk carton. "You'll need one, too."

"Need what?"

"For the raspberries." Her gray eyes looked straight into mine. She knew I had seen the matches. But as far as she was concerned what could a packet of matches possibly mean to me?

I took the carton and ran out the door and down the steps. "The Yangtze expedition leaves now!" I yelled at the top of my voice.

It was the only way to stop myself from crying.

Yang! Yang! Yang!

Amy and Clare and I bounced up and down in the early morning sunshine. We yelled the words to "Hang Down Your Head Tom Dooley." We yelled even louder as our ragged shouts ricocheted off the old railway tunnel and exploded over the trees.

"This is the best place in the world," screamed Amy. "I'm going to bounce here forever!"

"And ever and ever," shouted Clare.

Yang! Yang! Yang!

I bounced up and down beside them but it was as if I wasn't there. And I knew it was because of what I had found out from listening in the basement of Sandra's house.

My mother once told me how farmers cure their dogs of killing chickens. You tie a dead one around the dog's neck. By the time the chicken is so rotten that it falls off, the dog will never touch one again.

I knew something that had separated me from Amy and Clare. It felt like it was an invisible stinking chicken around my neck.

Yang! Yang! Yang!

"Where's Andrew?" yelled Amy.

"He's at Mr. Chevrolet's," I shouted.

Yang! Yang! Yang!

"Let's take him some raspberries," yelled Amy in a shrill voice.

I looked at her. Suddenly her face had gone bright red like it had up at the house when I'd mentioned Sandra Wilkins.

I saw Clare look quickly at her sister. Something passed between them that I didn't understand.

Before I could say anything, Amy swung her legs over the wire into the air.

"I'm crossing the Yangtze!" she shouted. Then she landed like a gymnast on the other side and ran through the high shining grass.

The wild raspberries grew in rambling thorny clusters along the embankment of the railway track and over the front of the crumbling tunnel. They were small and sweet and the red juice stained our fingers like ink. We filled our cartons in twenty minutes even though we ate twice as many as we picked. Then we sat in the tunnel and chewed our honey sandwiches in silence.

Mine was beginning to feel like a lump of rubber in my mouth. Usually Amy chattered like a sewing machine. And where Amy left off Clare picked up. But that afternoon the silence got more and more uncomfortable as we each pretended to listen to the sounds going on outside the tunnel. The chittering of chipmunks. The squawk of a blue jay. The rat-ta-ta-tat of a woodpecker digging for grubs in a tree.

Suddenly Amy picked up a piece of slate and threw it as hard as she could against the wall. It smashed and fell to bits on the ground.

"What do you really, really think of Mr. Chevrolet?" she said in a strangled voice, staring straight ahead of her.

"We mean really, really," said Clare.

It was just about the last question I had expected them to ask. But I was glad they didn't want to talk about the Wilkinses anymore.

"I think Mr. Chevrolet is really nice," I said, hesitantly. "I mean, he's always been really nice to us."

"Is that all?" said Amy, hollowly.

My skin prickled. I remembered the look that had passed between them as Amy jumped over the fence. Something was making them very unhappy and I had no idea what it was.

I felt more and more edgy. "And, um, my mum and dad really like him." I said. "And, um, Andrew really likes him."

I looked at Amy's pointed freckled face. "Why are you asking me?"

To my horror, her eyes filled with tears. She picked up another stone and threw it against the wall. "You tell her," she said to Clare.

Clare hunched her shoulders and leaned forward. "It's like this," she said. She turned and looked behind.

"Nobody's listening, you idiot," cried Amy. She rubbed her eyes with her fists. "Tell her."

Clare shook herself and blinked. She looked more like an owl than ever. "The thing is," said Clare, "we think Mr. Chevrolet is in love with Mum and, um, we think Mum hasn't noticed."

"And if she doesn't notice soon, he might give up," said Amy in a desperate voice.

"And we really, really like him," said Clare, quietly. "And we haven't had a dad for a long time."

I thought back to the time when I had asked them what it was like not to have a father. And how much I had regretted asking because immediately I knew the answer.

It was awful not having a father. It was one of the saddest things in the world. And all you could do was try not to think about it too much, otherwise you got sad all the time.

"So we don't know what to do," said Amy. This time she didn't bother to rub her eyes. Tears dribbled down her cheeks. "We even wrote to the lady who answers problems in the newspaper but she never wrote back."

"And anyway Mum would have opened the envelope," said Clare.

"So what are we going to do?" insisted Amy. "We don't want to make a mistake but if we don't do something soon, it will be too late."

Clare blinked her tawny owl eyes at me. "Do you think Mr. Chevrolet loves our mum, Nancy?"

The invisible chicken around my neck felt ten pounds heavier. What could I do? I couldn't tell them what I knew. It might wreck everything.

I stared at my feet, knowing I had to say something soon.

"Have you told anyone else?" I said, finally.

Amy and Clare shook their heads.

"We almost told Mrs. Somers," said Amy, "because she's Mum's best friend, but then she called us *impossible*." She took a deep breath but her voice cracked anyway. "We're not impossible, are we, Nancy? Mr. Chevrolet likes us, doesn't he, Nancy?"

Clare leaned over and put a small brown hand on her sister's knee. "The raspberries are going all gooey," she whispered.

"So what?" said Amy miserably.

"We were going to take some to Mr. Chevrolet," said Clare.

"How can we go to Mr. Chevrolet's and pretend everything is all right when it's not?" cried Amy. She started to cry again. "I *hate* pretending. It makes me feel *sick*."

I was desperately trying to work something out before I opened my mouth. If Mrs. Linklater had been away for a week, maybe she had stayed all that time with Mr. Chevrolet at the Riverview Motel. And that must mean she liked him as much as Amy and Clare thought *he* liked *her*. And if he liked her and she liked him . . .

But maybe that was all movie stuff. I wasn't sure of anything anymore.

"So what's your plan?" said Amy, fiercely. She stared at me. "You must have one. You're not talking."

I bit my lip. I wanted to say something that would make them feel better. But I couldn't think of anything. So I made it up and it came straight out of a movie.

"OK," I said. "This is what we'll do."

"Well?" said Amy.

"What?" said Clare.

"We'll go to Mr. Chevrolet's and give him some raspberries," I said. "You act normal and I'll watch for signs."

"What you do mean, *signs*?" said Amy.

My mind was in a flat spin.

"You know, shaky hands, shifty looks, sweaty palms." I shrugged hopelessly. "That sort of thing."

Clare looked at me. "So after we look for signs, then what do we do?"

"We can talk about it tomorrow," I replied quickly.

"What difference is tomorrow going to make?" asked Amy.

"A lot," I said. It was like some horrible maze. With every turning I was getting more and more lost. With every word I was turning into a bigger and bigger liar. And there wasn't anything I could do to stop it.

"So?" said Clare, impatiently. "What difference?"

I didn't have a reason. I made it up. "That'll give me time to talk to Andrew. Then we'll know what he thinks."

"Huh!" said Clare. "Andrew only thinks about Disneyland."

But Amy seemed satisfied. Her face cleared and she picked a raspberry out of her carton and popped it in her mouth. "Seen anything of Tracy Wilkins?"

"No," I almost shouted. "And I don't want to."

And before anyone had time to reply, I grabbed my carton and ran out of the tunnel.

"Last one's a loser!" I yelled as I leapt back over the Yangtze exactly as Amy had leapt over it.

"Wait for us!" yelled Amy and Clare.

But I wasn't waiting because I wasn't going to Mr. Chevrolet's house, I was going home. And I was running so fast that Amy and Clare wouldn't find out until they got to Mr. Chevrolet's on their own.

Thirteen

That night I lay in bed and stared at the ceiling. All I could think of was what Andrew had said late that afternoon when he came back from Mr. Chevrolet's house.

When I had got home, I'd gone straight to the swings down in the meadow behind our house. I had spent the rest of the afternoon swinging backwards and forwards. It made me feel better and sometimes as I plunged and soared I could almost forget the mess everything seemed to be in.

Andrew had had to shout a couple of times before I realized he was there. I dragged my feet on the ground and jerked to a stop.

"Why didn't you come?" said Andrew angrily. His face was white and pinched. "We waited for you."

He kicked the ground with his trainers. "Why didn't you come?" he said again.

I could feel my stomach shrink. Something had happened at Mr. Chevrolet's house and somehow it was going to be my fault.

"You were wrong about the garage," said Andrew abruptly. "The Linklaters' car didn't break down."

Tears welled up in my eyes. "I didn't say it broke down," I almost shouted. "*You* said it broke down. You said that's why they were there together and I believed you."

We stared at each other. But we might as well have been wearing blindfolds.

"OK," said Andrew. He sat down on the other swing. His voice was calmer. "OK. This is what happened. I'm helping Mr. Chevrolet clear out his shed."

"What?"

Mr. Chevrolet never cleared out his shed. A horrible thought crossed my mind. "He's not moving, is he?"

"Of course he's not," said Andrew, sharply. "Why would he paint the bedrooms if he was moving? He's just clearing out his shed. Like he's sorted his books. And he's put away his papers."

"I didn't know that."

"You would have if you'd shown up," said Andrew, his voice rising. "Anyway, then Amy and Clare show up and we sit around waiting for you."

"I *couldn't* come."

"Why not?"

"I'll tell you later," I mumbled.

"So then I ask Mr. Chevrolet what was wrong with the Linklaters' car," said Andrew as if he hadn't heard me. "Then Amy says you had asked her the same thing. She said their car never broke down."

Andrew kicked the ground. "So then I said, how come Mrs. Wilkins said her sister saw your mother and Mr. Chevrolet at the Riverview garage?"

I thought I was going to be sick.

"So Amy says, 'Who told you that?'"

I held my breath even though I knew what was coming.

"So I said, 'Nancy did.' Then Amy shouted, 'It's not true and why should Nancy know something we don't?'" Andrew stopped.

I held my head in my hands.

"What did Mr. Chevrolet say?" I whispered.

Andrew gave me a curious look. "At first he didn't say anything but his face went all serious. Then all he said was 'Ah, Mrs. Wilkins again. You mustn't listen to what Mrs. Wilkins says.'"

I opened my mouth to speak but Andrew jerked his hand at me and went on talking.

"Then Amy said Mrs. Wilkins was a bad person because she'd heard her mother telling Mum."

"Mum? What does Mum—"

"Wait," said Andrew, angrily. "Then Mr. Chevrolet stood up and said we should all go home."

Andrew stared at me. His eyes were wide and his face white. "He wasn't mad or anything. He just never talked like that before." He stopped and swallowed. "Then Amy started to cry."

He picked up a stone and threw it as hard as he could into the woods.

"Everything's ruined," he said in a choked voice. "Everything's ruined and I don't know why."

I thought of what Amy and Clare had told me in the tunnel. Of the plan I had made to discuss things with Andrew. Maybe between the two of us . . .

"Maybe everything's not ruined," I said hoarsely. "You see, I know—"

"Oh, shut up!" shouted Andrew. He jumped up and the swing jerked from side to side. "You don't know anything, Nancy! You just make everything up."

He pushed the swing as hard as he could. "And now you've messed everything up, too!"

I woke up clammy and shaking. Around me, my bedroom was strangely light and for a moment I thought it might be morning.

But it wasn't morning. It was still dark. The light was coming from behind the curtains. It was a pale yellow light as if there was a huge lantern hanging up outside the house.

I jumped out of bed. For the first time I realized there was a smell of smoke in the room. I ran over to the window and pulled back the curtains.

At the top of the road through the trees I could see an enormous bonfire.

At the top of the road through the trees . . .

It wasn't a bonfire. It was the Linklaters' house.

"Mum! Dad!" I screamed at the top of my voice, and ran into the hall.

There was no reply.

I screamed again. I crossed the hall and pulled open the door to their bedroom.

The bed was empty. Bedclothes lay in a tangled heap on the floor.

I screamed again at the top of my voice.

Andrew stumbled, blinking, into the hall. "What—"

"The Linklaters' house is on fire," I cried. "Their house is on fire. Mum and Dad aren't here!"

Andrew stared at me; then suddenly he woke up. "Jesus Chrrrist!" he shouted. "Hurry! We gotta go!"

"Where are Mum and Dad?" I wailed.

"They're up *there*, you idiot," shouted Andrew as he ran back into his room.

I pulled on some clothes and remembered to put on my shoes. A minute later, Andrew and I were out of the house and running up the road.

As we got closer, the light from the fire got brighter and brighter. The crackling of the flames was incredibly loud. Something crashed and sparks exploded in the air like fireworks.

"We have to find Mum and Dad," shouted Andrew.

"What about Amy and Clare?" I sobbed. I looked at the burning house and thought of their bedroom, the upended bedsteads, the stack of chairs in the corner.

It was all gone.

We turned down their path. In front of the house was a huge fire truck. Its light was flashing round and round. Firemen ran all over the place shouting. Two of them held a hose and sprayed a torrent of water at the huge flames. I had always imagined that once a fire hose got going, the torrent of water would put out the flames immediately. But it didn't seem to be making any difference at all.

"Come on," said Andrew, running along the path in front of me.

But I couldn't move. Further away from the house, there were lots of people. Dark shapes were carrying pieces of furniture and setting them up on the grass. There were a sofa and a table. A standard lamp stood between two chairs. It looked almost funny, a living room outdoors. In the light of the flames, I saw the tall outline of my father talking to the short, rounder shape of Mr. Chevrolet. My mother stood beside Mrs. Linklater. She had her arms around her shoulder. Mrs. Linklater's sewing machine was at their feet.

Someone pushed past me. It was Lawrence Murdoch's father. "Stay out of the way," he said, gruffly. "This is no place for kids."

"Amy and Clare," I shouted. "Where are Amy and Clare?"

"They're safe," said Mr. Murdoch. "Everyone's safe."

I turned to find Andrew but he wasn't there anymore. Mr. Murdoch caught me by the shoulder. "Go straight to your mother, Nancy," he said.

I nodded and stumbled through the bushes away from him. I wanted to find Amy and Clare. I looked over to my mother to see if Andrew was there yet. He wasn't. He must have gone looking for them, too.

I cut through the trees around the front of the house. In the red light of the fire engine, I saw another group of people. Mrs. Wilkins was standing beside Mrs. Murdoch. They were talking to a fireman. There was no sign of Sandra or Tracy or Lawrence.

And still no sign of Amy and Clare.

Then I thought of the old Studebaker.

The only problem was how to get to it without being found out. I went down on my hands and knees and crawled through the long grass about ten feet away from where Mrs. Wilkins and Mrs. Murdoch were standing.

As I tried to slither past, the fireman walked off and Mrs. Murdoch and Mrs. Wilkins moved away towards the long grass.

I froze. I was terrified that now their attention was away from the fire, they would hear me.

"Awful. It's just awful." It was Mrs. Wilkins's thin, tinkling voice. "And I'll bet my bottom dollar nothing was insured."

"Guess not," said Mrs. Murdoch. "Couldn't afford it, probably. Premiums have hit the roof. We've just had to take one out for Tom's apartment."

"I didn't know Tom had an apartment."

"Just bought one in Toronto," said Mrs. Murdoch. I could hear the pride in her voice. "It's for Lawrence when he graduates next summer. He's been offered a job with General Motors down there."

Mrs. Wilkins laughed her little laugh. "You must be so proud of him."

"We certainly are," said Mrs. Murdoch. "Tom set his heart on Lawrence going to college. Now he'll have a real future." She paused. "How's Tracy?"

"Dog-tired, poor girl," said Mrs. Wilkins with her high, tinkling laugh. "She's been helping me with the church picnic all day. There didn't seem any point in waking her."

"No point," agreed Mrs. Murdoch. "Lawrence is here with his father, of course. But men are more useful in these sorts of situations."

I lay in the grass wondering what Mrs. Murdoch would say if she knew the truth. That Lawrence would never finish college now. That he wouldn't get the job with General Motors. Instead he would be getting married to Tracy Wilkins. Because Tracy Wilkins was having his baby. Because Tracy Wilkins wanted to get out and Lawrence Murdoch was her ticket.

Poor Mrs. Murdoch. Whenever I'd heard her talking to my mother, it was always about their plans for Lawrence. She would say time and time again how they wanted to give him the chance they'd never had. So Mrs. Murdoch had cleaned offices and stacked supermarket shelves to put him through college.

"Sorry to disturb, you, ladies." It was Mr. Wilkins's voice. "Nothing like a fire to bring people together. Hello, Norma. How's Lawrence? We haven't heard of him in a while."

My heart went bang in my chest. How could Mr. Wilkins tell such a lie? The heavens should open and a bolt of lightning should turn him to stone.

"Lawrence is fine, thanks, Rick," said Mrs. Murdoch. "He and Tom are here somewhere. Awful thing."

"Awful," agreed Mr. Wilkins.

"There must be *something* we can do to help," said Mrs. Murdoch. "It's too bad just standing here chatting. I'm going to find Freya."

"I'll come with you," said Mrs. Wilkins. "I sent Sandra home to get a sweater. I'd better see how she is."

They moved away and I slithered through the grass. When I was far enough away, I bent double and ran.

The chrome back bumpers of the Studebaker were in front of me. I saw three heads in the backseat.

I walked up to the old car with my heart hammering in my chest. What do you say when someone's house is burning down?

I tapped on the window and opened the front door.

Amy and Clare and Andrew were sitting in the backseat.

I couldn't believe my eyes. They had a big bottle of Coca-Cola and a bag of crisps. They were laughing and even though Amy was crying, it was as if something wonderful had just happened.

Fourteen

I climbed into the front passenger seat and slammed the door. I stared at their flushed happy faces. "Where were you? What's going on?"

"Hi, Nancy," said Andrew. "I tried to find you but you'd gone." He held out the bottle of Coke. "D'you want some Coke?" Clare pushed over the bag of crisps.

Suddenly I felt really angry. How could they be laughing? "What are you doing?" I shouted. "I've been looking for you everywhere."

"We're celebrating," said Andrew in a tight, excited voice.

"Yeah!" cried Amy. "We're celebrating, that's what we're doing!"

I couldn't believe my ears. What on earth were they talking about? A house was burning down. Horrible things were happening.

"What do you mean, you're *celebrating*?"

It was Clare who spoke first. She leaned forward and grabbed my shoulder. "You were right, Nancy," she said. "It *was* Mum and Mr. Chevrolet outside the Riverview."

"They told us this evening!" cried Amy. "We went down to Mr. Chevrolet's house for supper and they told us!"

"That's why Mr. Chevrolet was so strange," said Andrew. "It was supposed to be a surprise and I almost wrecked it."

"What are you talking about?" I shouted. "What's a surprise?"

"They're getting married," cried Amy, laughing and crying at the same time. "They told us they were getting married."

"Mum explained everything, Nancy," said Clare in her low voice. "She said you can't get married to someone you don't know really well because getting married is such an important thing."

"So you have to have long talks," explained Amy. "And get things sorted out."

"So they did," added Andrew. "At the Riverview."

"That's where Mum was when we were with Mrs. Somers," explained Clare.

Andrew leaned forward and patted my shoulder. "I'm sorry I shouted at you at the swings," he said. "You didn't mess anything up."

My mind yammered like a speeded-up record. I

held my head in my hands. "But your house," I said. "Your house is burning down."

"Yeah," said Amy as if she was talking about something that was happening in Alaska.

"Mum discovered it," announced Andrew, proudly.

"What?"

"When she was walking the dogs this evening."

"But where were *you*?" I asked Amy and Clare.

"I've just told you," said Amy, laughing again. "We were having supper at Mr. Chevrolet's house."

"Look, Nancy," said Andrew, slowly. "It's like this. Mum discovers the fire. She runs home."

"Your dad calls our dad," said Amy.

"Amy!" cried Clare in a stunned voice.

"Well, he is going to be our dad, isn't he?" shouted Amy. "He is going to be our dad." Her voice rang like a huge joyful bell.

She started to bounce up and down. "Who cares about this old house? I don't care."

Beside her Andrew started to whoop with glee. "Don't you see, Nancy? That's why Mr. Chevrolet was painting his bedrooms. He was getting his house ready."

"And that's why our mum made him those curtains," said Clare, more slowly.

"Getting ready for what?" I said.

Amy and Clare burst out laughing. "For us, Nancy! For us," cried Clare. "We're moving into Mr. Chevrolet's house!"

My mind went back to the afternoon I had seen Mrs. Linklater making the curtains. I saw her rest her hand on the material. Her eyes looked dreamy and far-away. *She looked as if she was smiling at a baby.*

She must have been thinking of Mr. Chevrolet. Maybe that's what people looked like when they were thinking of getting married.

"Why aren't you saying anything, Nancy?" said Clare. "Don't you understand yet?"

"Don't you remember what we told you in the tunnel?" asked Amy.

"About Mr. Chevrolet liking Mum and Mum not noticing," added Clare kindly.

"It's a miracle," shouted Andrew. "Jesus Christ, Nancy! It's a miracle."

A huge roaring filled my head. It was the roar of the flames. It was the roar of the blizzard in the Linklaters' kitchen. The roar of getting caught up in the Wilkinses' horrible pretend lives. It roared round and round. Then suddenly it stopped and I began to cry.

"Yippee!" cried Amy. She reached over and hugged me. "See, everybody, Nancy understands now."

"Have some more Coke," said Andrew. "I've kept you some."

He held out the bottle. It was empty.

"Never mind," said Amy. She opened the door. "We'll get some more. Mr. Chevrolet's got lots."

We climbed out of the Studebaker and walked up towards the house. The big flames had died down. The fire hose must have finally put them out.

More adults were sitting down on the sofas and chairs in the outdoor living room. There was talking and laughing and the *chink* of glasses and bottles.

"Mum and Mr. Chevrolet must have told everyone," whispered Amy. She hugged herself with delight. "See, they're having a party."

We pushed through the long grass and came up to the fire truck. Its headlights were on but the red flashing light on the roof had been switched off.

At that moment, Sandra Wilkins came round the other side of the truck. In the beam of the headlights, her face was white and terrified. She looked as if she had just seen a ghost.

She looked as if it was *her* house that had burnt down.

"Something terrible's happened," she squealed. "Something really terrible."

I stepped back in the shadows. I didn't want anything to do with Sandra Wilkins ever again.

Clare stepped forward. "What's wrong, Sandra?" she said.

"What's happened?" said Amy.

"I don't know what to do," whispered Sandra. She rubbed her face with her fist. "I don't know whether I should tell you."

She held out her arm and opened her hand. Inside it was a piece of crumpled-up paper.

"I found this on the kitchen table," she said in a voice so quiet, we could hardly hear her. "Read it, Nancy."

I shook my head.

"What does it say?" asked Andrew. He took it from her hand and held it in front of the fire truck's headlights.

Then he read aloud.

Dear Mum and Dad, Lawrence and me have gone to Disneyland. We're keeping our baby and we aren't coming back. Tracy. P.S. Sandra can have my pink blouse.

"See," said Andrew, triumphantly. He looked at Amy, Clare and me. "What did I tell you all along?"

I watched Amy and Clare staring openmouthed at Sandra's tear-stained face.

"You mean Tracy's *pregnant*?" gasped Amy.

Sandra sniffed and looked at me. "What's that?"

I ignored her. A huge weight had floated off my shoulders. For the first time since this horrible mess began, everyone knew what I knew. Now there were no more secrets. No more misunderstandings. It was as if we were all back to where we had started at the beginning of the summer.

Well, not quite. Some things had changed. It was great about Mrs. Linklater and Mr. Chevrolet. But I had a feeling the Wilkinses might not be neighbors for too much longer.

We stood and looked over to where the adults were talking. Their circle of chairs and sofas was lit by the burning remains of the house. Mr. Chevrolet had his arm around Mrs. Linklater's waist. It sounded as if he was making a speech. We heard Mrs. Wilkins's high, tinkling little laugh and the gruff guffaw of Lawrence Murdoch's father.

"Wow!" muttered Andrew to himself. "They could be halfway there by now."

Amy stared at him. "What are you talking about?"

Andrew rolled his eyes. "Disneyland, of course." He paused. "Are you dumb, or something?"

Clare and Amy and I looked at each other. We couldn't help it. We started to giggle. Soon we were holding on to each other and rolling around, sobbing with laughter.

Beside us Sandra sniffed and wiped her nose with her sleeve. "I don't see what's so funny!" she squealed. "What am I going to *do*?"

"Look," said Andrew as kindly as he could since he had never liked Sandra much. "What you have to do is this." He handed Sandra back her letter. "Just tell your parents nicely and maybe they'll take *you* to Disneyland next year."